Happenstance

Happenstance

First Galleon Edition, November 2025
ISBN 978-1-998122-27-1

Published by Galleon Books
Moncton, New Brunswick, Canada
www.galleonbooks.ca

Cover art "Sheet Music" by Pamela Marie Pierce.

This is a work of fiction. Names, characters, businesses and events are a product of the author's imagination and any resemblance to real-life individuals or events is purely coincidental. Place names are real; however, events described are fictional. Some surnames are real; the characters bearing those surnames are fictional.

Warning: This novel deals with the trauma of sexual abuse and suicidal ideation.

Suicide Crisis Helpline

9-8-8 Suicide Crisis Helpline (Canada)
www.988.ca
A safe space to talk, 24 hours a day, every day of the year.
Call or text 9-8-8
If your safety is at risk, call 9-1-1 right away.

Library and Archives Canada Cataloguing in Publication

Title: Happenstance / Thomas Chamberlain.
Names: Chamberlain, Thomas (Retired teacher), author.
Identifiers: Canadiana 20250319926 | ISBN 9781998122271 (softcover)
Subjects: LCGFT: Novels.
Classification: LCC PS8605.H33935 H37 2025 | DDC C813/.6—dc23

Happenstance

Thomas Chamberlain

GALLEON

Dedication

To all those in prisons of body and soul, in bad relationships, and addictions; may your hearts be open to find a way.

For the medical and psychological caregivers; may you have the strength to carry out your roles.

For all the parents; may you have the endurance to love your children unconditionally.

Johnny Buck 1968 – 2024

To all the students, teachers, friends, and family that helped find my voice.

1

The Last Time

There's a rustling behind me. Cold air flows in over my shoulders. My eyes focus on glowing red numbers: 1:47.

Gin fumes waft through my hair and wrap around my head. I hear the hollow sound of air through nostrils, whiskers burn my naked neck, a heavy leg slips between mine. Hands search through the sheets and come up under my nightgown. My nipples are pinched, my breasts are squished against my chest. Nostrils roar and the odour makes me nauseous.

Through my window: a plane races across the stars. The blinking light pulls me into the empty jet. I look down, searching the earth for bedroom lights. I wonder how many people are looking up wishing they were on this flight.

The pressure eases from my chest. My lungs expand. I lay my head flat on the pillow. Warm slime runs between my legs. Fingers pull hair back over my temple. Lips and whiskers press a kiss on the back of my head.

"I love you, Darby."

"I love you too."

The mattress rises. The door opens and closes. I look back out the window: the plane has gone. I am damp and cold. The red numbers say 1:58.

I use a facecloth to soak up the wet puddle in the middle of my bed. I pull the sheets off, rinse the cloth and throw it all in the laundry.

This is the last time.

I turn on the shower, and step in. My hand deflects the water until my body can accept the scalding spray. The bar of soap follows every curve, from fingertips to toes. I wipe stickiness from between my legs, pull the shower curtain over and throw the facecloth into the hamper. Hanging my head in the flow, my hair forms a tunnel. Lines of soap run around my legs like serpents, washing him away.

The ghosts of his fingers press against my breasts. I was twelve when Mom and I went bra shopping. She told me I was a beautiful, intelligent girl, and now I was becoming a beautiful, intelligent woman. She said you cannot stop nature and genetics. She told me she bought her first bra when she was twelve. She kissed me warm and soft on the forehead. I could feel the lipstick make a seal between her lips and my head. She left her lips there for a second. When she pulled away, her eyes brimmed.

Sara told me I was lucky that I would have my mother's curves, my mother who Sarah said was the M.I.L.F. in the neighbourhood and would look beautiful wearing nothing but a shower curtain. She, however, was probably going to stay as straight-legged and flat-chested as her mom. She was thirteen and still waiting for something to happen. Sara was right. She has long muscles that flex and twist with her movements. I'm round, with a layer of fat that gives me soft shapes.

Lucky? Not.

Dad said his teenage daughter should have her own room in the basement where she could play her music, practice her saxophone, and tie trout flies. There would be peace upstairs in the house then.

Dad and I screwed down the subfloor. I lined up every screw into an imaginary chessboard pattern. I steadied the studs on plumb for the air gun, pushed and pulled wires through the holes, and hung the sheetrock. I rubbed my finger over each screw to feel its dimple. The night before the crack filler came, in a jam jar, I put a Muddler Minnow fly, a picture of Mom and me holding a trout I caught, and two flakes of chert that a Stone Age native had scraped off forming an arrowhead. I added a picture of Sara and me standing in our Sherrie and Terri costumes that we wore on twin day in Grade Seven. Through an outlet hole, I dropped it behind the wall; it hit the floor plate with a clunk. It would be there forever. It was the beginning of the end. I didn't know at the time, but maybe I did?

It took me a month, looking at paint chips and fabric swatches, to make up my mind. We rolled five test-paint patches on the wall. Mom, Sara and I painted the walls "Soft Rose Red." We bought a wrought iron bed at the Habitat for Humanity store. I positioned it three times until I could see the stars from my pillow. Mr. Simms gave me a music stand from school as well as a sax stand. Mom and I found a wooden desk at Past Perfection; it was strong and solid. Its nicks and dings made my mind wander to what creations it had aided, and the indent from my fly-tying vise would add to the patina.

Sara said she wished she had her own pad in the basement. Mine even has a washer and dryer, like it was my own apartment. I wouldn't move in until everything was complete.

I asked Dad if Sara could spend the night, and he said she could. It was the first day of Christmas vacation in Grade Seven, and Sara brushed make-up on my face. We slept with our cold feet intertwined.

That New Year's Eve, the monster came to visit.

I knew him well, but this was the first time he visited my room at home. He stood by my bed. I reached between the folds of his housecoat for his cock. As matter-of-factly as telling me to hold the stud steady for the air nailer, he said, "Now you're a woman and ready to show love like one." He flopped me over like a sod at the end of a shovel. I knew what was going to happen; it was like a progression of events in a horror movie and you know the killer is hiding in the closet. You don't want that door to open but you know it has to for the plot to continue. The hands that held me steady on my new bike when I was five, now gripped and pulled my hips up. I wanted to say no. Instead, I turned my head and looked out the window. The moon was in its first quarter, Mars a red jewel at its tip. I let it pull my soul from my pillow to a place in-between here and there.

When my soul came back, Dad was gone. I was a mess of crumpled sheets, the smell of gin, tears, and cold slime. I lay in bed, my body shaking, tears leaking out of my eyes, realizing the room was not mine at all.

I change the bed, crawl between my new sheets, kick my feet to loosen them, and breathe in the freshness. The red numbers say 3:30. I close my eyes. Three hundred, two hundred and ninety-nine, two hundred and ninety-eight, two hundred and ninety-seven.

Ping, ping, ping, on the pane. The stars are gone. I pray school isn't cancelled. I have a math test in six hours. I realize it doesn't matter anymore.

Two hundred and ninety-six, two hundred ninety-five, two hundred ninety-four, two hund…

2

The Plan

A plan was necessary to end the terror. The tormented had to make a permanent change to end the tormentor's reign. By leaving, the monster would be defeated and left to wither, deprived forever.

Like any good plan, it didn't come together instantly. Two years of thoughts, ideas, options and dates. My first best plan was to save five hundred dollars, then withdraw it, mail a note to Sara, and leave in the middle of the night. May 23. I'd walk to the wharf, put all my stuff in a canoe, paddle the boat out into the river, weigh myself down with a 10-kilo anchor, and go over the side. I knew the dark silt that filled the Kennebecasis would never give me up, and eels would eat my remains. Mom wouldn't ever have to know. I hung on to that plan. But then I realized that Sara would never stop looking for me. She would be forever spotting me in crowds. I read about a mom who jumped every time the phone rang after her daughter went missing. They would need closure so after the sorrow they could move on. Mom is only thirty-four. Dad agreed to let her work at Cards and Roses, and she loves it. Sara has friends; she'll become a doctor and travel the world. I can see her in one of those UNICEF commercials holding a big-eyed, brown-skinned baby.

Actually, I had three hundred and sixty dollars saved at that time; babysitting money Dad paid me for taking care of Davey when he and Mom went out to parties. He always came home drunk. I have the sounds memorized.

The truck enters the garage, motor shuts off, muffled voices in the kitchen, two toilet flushes, water pump clicks on, water pump clicks off, silence, feet on my stairs, door opens… In the morning two twenty-dollar bills on the counter. At first, I didn't want the money. Mom says Dad suggested it, because if he didn't pay me, he'd have to pay someone else. I have never spent a single dollar of that fuck money. Now I have sixty twenty-dollar bills.

The wind whips against the house, making the siding crackle and shift. I hear my breathing.

"Darby, it's time," Mom stands on the low tide shore in her bathrobe. A curtain of fog covers her, then reveals her. "Darby, Darby it's time to come home."

"Yes, I know. I'll be right there." The rope uncoils over the side.

I'm sitting up looking at the red numbers: 4:31. My heart is pounding a strong beat. It seems like years since my mind has slept. I get up. The sleet falls in slanted parallel lines through the lighted cone cast by the neighbour's back-door light.

I go back into the bathroom and I get on the scale: 112 lbs. Someone's going to notice.

I climb up on the toilet and shim one of the hanging tiles from the ceiling. Reaching up, I grab the plastic bag and slide the tile back in place. Stepping down, I wipe up the grey dust that has settled on the tank then unzip the bag and dump it onto my bed. Pills and a wad of twenties bounce on the mattress.

It was a windy night in March; Mom and Dad were out and I was babysitting. While Davey slept, I snooped through Dad's dresser. I remember being really really quiet, as if he was in the house. I found a prescription bottle tucked in the bottom drawer where he keeps his big heavy wool socks. I knew he was hiding them from Mom. I spilled the pills on the bed and counted them – 32. It was the first time I stole something and I didn't know why. It was like the jam jar; a plan was taking shape before I consciously had my first thoughts. I Googled, *benzodiazepine,* sleeping pills. By Grade Nine I had stolen nine. That's when I decided I would need 20 in order to leave.

I remember lying in bed, rolling the pill between my finger and thumb, and deciding every time the monster came, I would steal a pill. After the fifth visit, I could see the pattern of one more pill being gone, like someone had been in the bottle before me. I continued stashing pills. If he suspected, I thought, he'd move the bottle. And when the bottle got down to five pills, I'd stop until the refill.

I count them, lining them up in five rows and four columns, same count as yesterday. As planned. Twenty.

In two days, it will be the first Saturday in February; the day I picked for leaving. It will never be on a long weekend because there's no holiday in February. Valentine's Day was my only concern but it will never be the first Saturday and it is pretty much a fluff day anyway. I will not be a memory during anyone's summer holiday, birthday or anniversary.

Davey's hockey schedule this weekend puts him and Dad in St. Stephen at a tournament. Mom works the Saturday a.m. shift at Cards and Roses. I will have the house to myself.

Either Dad's truck or the ATVs will be in the garage. I already checked the gas tanks.

Mom will find me. She'll think I'm sleeping. Then she'll realize I'm gone and rock me in her arms, tears spilling out of her eyes. I couldn't let the monster tell her the news.

I put the pills back in the bag and shove it up under the ceiling tile. I wipe the toilet tank again. I stuff the twenties in my backpack. I line up my shoes so all the heels touch the second seam of hardwood planks inside my closet. Back between the sheets, I see rain streaking down the glass. The red numbers say 5:11. My eyes search for a pattern in the indentations on the ceiling tiles as I wait for the house to come alive.

"OK Darby, keep it in the center of the road. You're doing fine," Dad says.

I look through the steering wheel. Tires crackle over the gravel road. His hands hold me in place from behind. My hands vibrate with the steering wheel.

"OK, let's stop."

Dad's chest heaves against my back. He lifts me and puts me back in my place – "shotgun." He looks down to where I was sitting, on his lap. A long stick with a purple top sways at his waist.

"What's wrong, Dad?"

"Nothing. I love you so much. You made this happen. It won't go away unless you touch it."

My outstretched fingers touch the tip. He groans. I look up at his face and down at my hand which is all covered in warm eel slime.

"I want you to never forget that this is a special love between me and my special girl. Mom can't make this happen for me. It makes me so happy that you can. If Mom knew that you made Dad so happy and she couldn't, she would be very sad. She would leave and never come back. This is our fishing-trip secret. OK, Darby?

"Darby, Darby."

"Yes, I hear you. OK, OK, I'm up."

"Time to get ready; I don't think school's going to be cancelled," Dad's voice comes from the other side of the door. I hear Davey banging his hockey bag against the wall as he lugs it up the stairs. The red numbers say 6:02. It's still dark outside. I lay in bed listening for the Jeep to leave the garage.

I remember washing up in the creek. I didn't ask why Mom would be upset, but asked if Mom leaves am I going with her or staying with you, and Dad saying, "Mom doesn't have a job. She couldn't keep you. If you left with her, you'd have to change schools." I know I was four, because Mom was in the hospital having Davey, and this was our special trip before she came home that afternoon. It is the earliest memory I can identify with an age. I don't remember thinking anything else. For years it was go fishing, drive the truck, grab the stick – although I remember sometimes the stick needed to be rubbed a bit – wash up and everyone was happy. I remember one day coming home from fishing and Mom was sitting in the rocker crying. I was sure she knew. I went to my room, lay in bed and prayed, and promised God I'd be a good girl if he didn't let Mom know.

3

Getting Out of the House

√ Earrings
√ Hug
√ Supper plans
√ Saxophone
√ Library Books
√ Clean out Locker
√ Skip History/Money/ letter
  Lunch Sara/Lori
  Mr. Frank
  Necklace
  Mail letter
  Supper
  Sara
  Breakfast Hug
  Clean/ Laundry
  Leave

I swing my feet out of bed. Being up is a relief; I can control my thought patterns.

I pick up the feathered earrings I made from pheasant hackle and head upstairs to Mom. She's wrapped up in her big brown terry housecoat.

"Good morning, Sunshine. I was sure school would be cancelled when I got up and looked out the window. The buses are an hour late. I have some waffles in the toaster," Mom says as she pushes the handle down.

I hold up the earrings. "Listen, I made these for you. You can wear them when you're goofin' around." Mom sets down her coffee, takes the gift and holds them at eye level. They match her brown eyes and chestnut hair. She smiles. I smile back.

"Thank you, they're beautiful." She gives me a big hug. I wrap myself around her. Squeezing, I breathe her in. Lips press against my head. I hang on, wanting to feel her for a few more seconds. Her arms loosen around me as she leans back and combs my hair with her fingers. "Are you OK, sweetheart?"

What do I say? Dad has been banging me for the last three years in the basement. I haven't slept in years. I thought Dad's erection was a sign of love. I'm the forty-dollar whore in the cellar. I don't wear make-up because Dad has this whole set of rules. I keep secrets to keep us together, and telling the truth is more complicated than just saying good-bye.

I avoid Dad the morning after, so I have to think up a lie to get out of the house before he returns in an hour with Davey.

"Yeah, I'm fine. I'm runnin' to Sara's before the bus. She has a math test and she'll have questions."

"Are you sure, babes? It's raining and blowing a gale. You'll get soaked."

"If I do, I'll borrow something from Sara. Mom, can we make pizza for supper? I'll cut up the stuff before you get home."

"Sure, sweetheart, I'm done at five," Mom says.

"Great. Love you."

"I love you too, sweetie."

I had a dress picked out, but I go with jeans, a white, collared shirt and a beige sweater that hangs down below my ass. Messy bun. Conceal as much as possible. Special daughters are not to flaunt their shape otherwise they'll be known as easy. Dad hasn't been in a high school lately. Earrings are allowed. Make-up is in my locker and at Sara's. I have to wear some to keep the roving packs of She Wolves at school thinking I am half normal. I check my agenda. I think I am the only one on the planet not connected. I knew better than to ask.

I lift my sax up out of its stand, twist off the mouth-piece, replace it with the one it came with and case it up. In the top drawer, I fumble through socks. I know where the ones I want are. Unfolding the ball, I find the gold chain in the toe. Sara brought it back from Jamaica for me when she was in Grade Nine. It was my first piece of gold, and I remember how cold it felt the first time I put it on. It lay flat against my skin; as I twisted and turned, it caught the light and shimmered. I knew there would be questions about where I got it, or maybe I would not be allowed to wear it. Mom has never seen it. I put the chain around my neck and down my shirt.

The weather has caused a small glitch. Mom will make a fuss if she sees me going out with it in the storm. I decide to wait for the water pump to come on. I place my finger between the hangers in my closet to keep the even spacing. The water pump finally whines to life. She's in the shower.

4

Trapped

I grab a garbage bag, wrap up my sax and tie a knot. Shoes, no sneakers. I wear my backpack, sling my purse, cradle the sax under my arm and pull the black-and-white umbrella out of the vase beside the door. The wind yanks the front door from my hand. I turn back and push it closed with my hip, set down the sax and slide the umbrella to the click. I lean the hemisphere against the wind; the rain hits it like machine gun fire. Umbrella ahead of me, my feet follow the tire tracks down the driveway and onto the road. I stay in the tracks to keep out of the slush; one foot in front of the other, on a tightrope. I use my hip to heave my sax higher under my arm so I can use two hands to steady the umbrella. Two blocks and a turn to Sara's.

Honk, honk. I jump and my foot sinks into the slush. The umbrella bobbles, spins me in the opposite direction and pulls me down the street. My sax hits the ground and I stagger after the runaway umbrella like an owner with a bad dog. *Swish!* The umbrella inverts; I stumble to a stop. Dad is going to kill me. My purse dangles from my elbow. I look back for my sax. It is held by a man standing by the smoking tailpipe of a blue car.

"You need a hand? I am so sorry for startling you," he yells.

"I think I'm fine."

He starts walking towards me. I just stand there trying to figure out how to fix the umbrella.

"Let me see that." I hand over the umbrella because I guess he'll know the trick to reshape it. "It died a brave soldier," he says. In one step and swoop he stabs it handle down in the snowbank, and snaps a salute to the flips and flaps of nylon and bent wire.

I look down to hide a silly smile. "I guess it fought its last battle," I say, looking up at his furry bombardier hat's ear flaps waffling in the wind.

"Here are your choices: you can continue down the road in the rain, or jump in and I'll give you a lift back home since the buses are an hour late. If you wish, I'll give you a ride to either Rothesay or Kennebecasis Valley High. I teach at K.V. I'll take the river road if you want to go to Rothesay, but we should do something 'cause we're startin' to look like two fools too dumb to come in out of the rain," he says, shifting the sax from one arm to the other.

I look up. I wipe wet hair away from my face, swallow rainwater flowing over my lips. "I think I'll take the drive." He nods, then turns and walks to the car. He opens the door, leans in and lays my sax on the backseat. He opens the passenger door.

I walk to the car thinking of Davey driving by looking at the dead umbrella, saying, "Dad what's our umbrella doing in the snowbank?" And Dad replying, "You sure it's ours?" And as soon as he gets in the house, checking the back porch where the umbrella should be and realizing the worst, yelling "shit" upstairs to Mom for letting me have it.

Mom shouting back, "What are you yelling about?"

Finally, he'll march outside and, cursing, pull it out of the snowbank like he was rescuing his child from the cold.

I sink down into the seat and pull the door closed. Warm air from the vents covers me like a blanket. I'm riding with a complete stranger, but the car isn't moving. I turn my head; the furry hat is gone.

"Tom Buckley," he says, as he extends his hand. I've never shaken hands before. I reach out.

"Darby... Saunders."

"Well, Miss Saunders, we are no longer strangers. Do you want me take you back home?"

"No."

"Which school – Kennebecasis or Rothesay?"

"Kennebecasis."

The car starts to roll. I look over. My eyes go to his crotch. I feel embarrassed. I turn my gaze back out the windshield. Do I tell him I am going to Sara's? Will he think I'm scared of him if I do? Holy shit, there's our truck coming up the street! Davey's head is turned, talking to Dad. I duck below the dash and brush imaginary slush off my sneakers. I retie one.

"I think I should've worn my boots," I say.

"Well, it's hard to look stylish in the halls with rubber boots on," he replies. "I have never seen you in the halls. What grade are you in, Darby?"

I look up. We've passed Sara's street. "Ten." I am trapped. He looks over and shifts the car up into third.

"My wife took a transfer here from Halifax, so I just started there this semester," he says. "My room is down in the one hundreds. I haven't even had a chance to learn the names of my own students yet. I assume you live on the block?" he says.

"Yeah, I can see your backyard from our house. I'm two up on Maplecrest. Your backyard and ours meet at the vertex, so-to-speak. I sometimes see your Bernese Mountain Dog inside your fence."

"Sasha. She is a big baby more than a big dog. You have a dog?"

"No. Dad's allergic to them." The wipers swipe the rain off the windshield. The highway is one plowed lane and one with two tire tracks. A passing transport truck sprays us with slush and slops the windshield. There's silence while the windshield wipers catch up. I think of all the times I thought of reaching over and pushing the wheel into the path of a truck. I practiced timing it in my mind. The risk of one of us surviving was too great. My current plan has no risk.

"I kinda thought school would be cancelled and we'd be able to unpack some more stuff. What's your dad do?"

"He's a lawyer," I say, looking out the passenger window. What do I ask? I already know the small answers because Sara told me: his name, his room, his classes; that he's "hot for thirty-something," married, from Halifax. I told her about the dog, and that his wife drives a Jag and dresses to match, which trumped all her info. Do I ask why we're in a Corolla? No. I settle for "What classes are you teaching?"

"Well, Grade Nine – Math and English," he says, keeping his eyes on the road. "What kinda brass do you play? No, let me guess, a straight pipe? No, no, you look like a girl with more swing; an alto sax?"

My head turns to him. His has already turned, antici-pating my surprise. His whiskers are a black mass indented in his face, outlining a perfect beard template. Am I staring? There is a smile, but no teeth show through. I have nowhere else to look and nothing to say. I become conscious of my idle hands.

"I'm not psychic. Last Saturday night I was standing in the backyard with Sasha. All was silent, but, faintly, I could hear noodling from an alto sax. It was very soft, kind of haunting. Then the noodling turned into *Tupelo Honey*. Out 'woodshedding' at two a.m. You were playing some serious chops girl!"

I can feel a blush on my cheeks. I swallow. His eyes are back on the road. "You're not a beginner, are you?"

"The sax, for three or four years now… piano since I was six. You play?"

"Yep, used to play in a cover band, The Blue Tones. We did some original stuff as well. I was younger then. You plan to play professionally?"

The thought never crossed my mind and I realize I have no goal to my playing. Probably a good thing – I'm turning in the sax today. "I never really thought about it," I say.

"Well, you should. A good sax player that can read music, could play their way through college by sitting in with this band and that, being a studio musician, teaching, or busking," he says. "And you're on your way to being good enough." He hits the signal light.

I glance over. We're taking the wrong exit.

"Since we're not in a hurry this morning, I'm stopping for a coffee. You a coffee girl? I'm buying."

"I'm fine. You don't have to."

"Yeah, I know I don't, but I want to."

We ease into the lineup.

"Look, we're here with all the other caffeine addicts. So, what can I get you to make your day a little less rainy?" When I hesitate, he nudges me. "Let's decide; this is a jittery bunch behind us."

"Good morning. What can I get for you?"

Hot chocolate, or coffee? I order Mom's usual: "A double-double, please."

"One large coffee, black, and a large double-double. That's two eighty-five."

We roll forward to the next window and he pays. He passes me my first coffee.

"There you go, Darby."

My fingers brush against his as I take the cup. I look down and glance into his lap.

"Shit!" he says. I look up. He's licking coffee from the back of his hands. "Will you grab this for a second?" He passes me his coffee and starts wiping coffee off the steering wheel and wringing the napkin in his hands. "Thanks." He reaches back for the cup. I peel back my lid, careful not to cause a mess. "Excuse me for swearing," he says.

"Your wife has a nice car," I say, wanting to take my words back as soon as they leave my mouth.

"You saw the car. She looks like a Philadelphia lawyer driving that. Actually, it was an inheritance from her grandfather. Don't spread that around the neighborhood." A wink. "She likes the mystique the car brings. She produces commercials and does P.R. work."

We turn into the faculty parking lot and back into a space. Looking through the windshield, I see the tires have cut a grey parallel signature into the snow. "I think I can sneak you in here this morning," he says as we climb out. I set my coffee on the roof, reach into the backseat for my stuff. "I got it," he says, pulling my sax through the door on his side before I have a chance to grab it.

I lead the way to the door and wonder what he's thinking behind me. Too helpless to carry my own stuff? Stupid for coming to school early? A lonely loser blowing air into a brass pipe at two in the morning instead of being out at a party? Is he looking at my ass? I stop in front of the *Faculty Entrance,* and try to figure out how to shift my purse, knapsack and coffee to open the door. I feel stupid for making us stand in the rain. He reaches around me. I can see the dark hair on his fingers and a gold band slightly embedded into his skin.

"Let me get that." The door swings open and I step forward. "You want me to take this to the cafeteria for you?" he asks.

"No, just set it here and I'll come right back for it."

"OK then. You're the boss." He kicks the wall, knocking the snow from his boots "Have a great day, Darby!"

I look into his blue eyes. "You too, Mr. Buckley. Thanks for the drive and the coffee."

"It was a pleasure."

5

Getting Started

R36-L24-R12 I pull the lock down and open the door.

I pick my coffee up off the floor and set it on my locker shelf. I rip the bag and take my sax out, cross the hall and push the wet bag through the swinging door of the garbage can. I drag the can over to my locker; lift the top off so I don't have to listen to the squeaking of the lid. I'm glad to be here in a desolate locker room, free from prying eyes, but I realize the only one that would ever ask what I was doing was Sara.

I throw out a box of pads. Dad tracks my menstrual cycle, like a dog smelling a bitch in heat. The Pill was never an option since the Sexual Health Nurse would ask too many questions and I wasn't sure I could lie to her. I thought about dating Barry. He's spent his two years in Grade Eleven selling crack and fucking Grade Nine and Ten girls who are desperate for acceptance, think drugs are sexy, or just want to trade. With him, less fucking would be easier. Had Mom met him – his beard, his jeans, his tattoo and his car – the Pill would not be a problem. Explaining Barry to Sara would be, though, especially after I've refused all of her boyfriend suggestions. If Dad found out I had a boyfriend, or was on the Pill, I'd be locked up. He's not sharing. Every month, I timed my period to the day. The late days, I cried and played my sax; one night I tied fifty #6 Adams Dry Flies. I went to the bathroom every class. I couldn't say I had a boyfriend or I was raped or it was Immaculate Conception. Mom would die. I had to leave.

I rifle through my textbooks, looking for paper notes and pulling off stickies. I place the textbooks up on the top shelf, tallest to shortest left to right.

My assignment binder hits the bottom of the can with a thud. I look around to see if I've drawn any attention. Two kids are sitting up against their lockers at the end of the hall, looking my way.

I slide all my scribblers into my backpack. I'll ditch them one period at a time. I pull the mirror off the inside of the door. After untying my sneakers, I peel off my soaked socks and push my bare feet into my gym shoes. I toss the wet ones into the locker… but who'd want used sneakers? Into the garbage they go. I take my make-up bag, science text, and *To Kill a Mockingbird*, and place my sax in the bottom of my locker. I slam the door, hook the lock, twirl the dial.

In the washroom, I shake out my bun. I pull the brush through what Mom refers to as "a pony's mane." She has brushed sand, burdocks, gum and cooties out of it. I've never been called a ginger. I'm a natural deep rich amber and in its folds, it's almost black. My hair is thick; it pleats and shapes itself. It hides my face when I tip my head forward. In my child photos, I am the kid with the mop. Sara says it's a beacon for guys, and the envy of straight-haired brunettes. I have never really cut it. Dad likes it long. I was going to crop it as a statement, but I figure Mom has never seen me any other way. I don't want her to be scared when she finds me. I just want her to hold me.

Last time Mom brushed it was in January. Dad was away. Mom wandered into my room, slipped the brush from my hand and said, "Let me do that for you." She sat on my bed and pulled, tugged, and stroked my hair. I could smell wine. I never turned around. My heart was thumpity-thumping and I started to feel sweat roll down from my armpits along my ribs. I had so much I wanted to say. Maybe I was waiting for her to start. Why didn't she ask, "Why were you doing laundry last night?" or, "Did you hear Dad in the basement last night? Do you have a boyfriend? Why didn't you go to Jessica's party with Sara? If you want to start taking the Pill, let me know." When I lay down to sleep, she lay behind me. I could feel the weight and warmth of her body. When I woke, she was gone.

I look in the mirror, smooth on some foundation, blush my cheeks, moisten my lips with my favourite ochre gloss and brush up my lashes. Leaving the washroom, I push the make-up bag into the waste basket.

The halls are full. The PA system starts blabbing the day's schedule changes. The upper lobby is a staging area that looks like a mass of kids. To an untrained eye, it's a mob. To students, it is an organized hierarchy. Cool kids are in the centre around the benches, then it spreads out to the usual groups that are visible: BFFs, EMOS, TEAMMATES, GOTHS, GAYS, STUDY GROUPS, WANNABES. Then there are the POOR, HUNGRY, ABUSED, DEPRESSED, LONELY; not so easily recognized because they are in distant hallways, under stairs, in classrooms, huddled in the woods or right in the midst of the group.

I weave, turning my shoulders, navigating the crowd and finally pushing into the library. The doors push back as if making entry a commitment. I like the library. You can appear to have friends because there are always people at the tables, some working, some trying to fake belonging.

"Good morning, Darby."

"Good morning, Mrs. Connors. I want to return these books," I say, pulling two novels out of my backpack. I place the books on the counter.

"Have you seen our new arrivals? I just unpacked them." I look behind me at the table and stare at books that have been stood strategically on the new arrival table. The lucky ones will have their pages soiled and dog-eared, tiny rips will appear at the edges of their dust covers. They will be taken to private places, talked about, held close to people's hearts in the special hour between awake and asleep, while others will languish on the table until they are slid back into the Dewey Decimal System. They will suffer an endless high school career of obscurity and loneliness, while they sit inches away from what they want. I won't do that.

"I'll have to check them out later Mrs. Connors. Thanks for taking time," I say. I don't look back to acknowledge her acceptance of my compliment.

<h1 style="text-align:center">6</h1>

Waiting for Sara

My morning assemblage is a dozen girls on the floor in a U-cove of lockers. Like a group of boys at a middle-school dance, we avoid any eye contact that may lead to an encounter. Of the student body, we are the hydrogen: colourless, odourless, tasteless, nontoxic and highly flammable. We sit in every class, walk the halls; mostly disguised in the compounds of a multitude of cliques. Our repulsive forces exceed our attractive ones. We like it that way. We have no dates. Insecure high school boys won't date girls who can take hydrogen out of Chemistry and into English class.

Our combined marks could probably be split up to pass the entire boys' football team.

We are no threat to the "She Wolves." We don't display cleavage, show skin above the knee, stand in public places, or have *juicy* written across the ass of our sweatpants. We don't giggle and shake as we scuff our feet in the halls as an auditory indicator of our approach.

We are careful not to voice any social opinion.

In class, we sit in the front against the wall, speaking only when spoken to. We never disagree with student comments; project our voices to reach the teachers' ears only.

We are the chorus, recognizable only to mothers, but necessary so even minor actors have someone to be compared with.

I took the extra precaution of lowering my marks to ninety. Good, but not exceptional.

Hall traffic has picked up. Sara will get off the bus and meet with the volleyball girls down by the gym to discuss boys, and because I wasn't at the bus stop, she'll come down here to find out why. I've never missed a day.

I sit and lean back on my locker. I pop a CD in my Discman and put my headphones on. My eyes close; my ears fill with Charlie Parker's sax.

It was the second day of school. Mom said I was a big girl; I could walk to the bus stop myself, and that both the bus stop and the bus were sort of a classroom where I would learn stuff. I wouldn't make friends holding her hand. Mom was right.

The bus stop had as many parents as kids. I stood looking in the direction of the bus's approach. I repeated the lines over and over: *get on first bus, get off at the second school, the one with the big trees.* A truck that sounded like Dad's pulled up to the curb. I thought Dad had come to wait with me, but when I looked up, it was a blue truck. A girl with a pink backpack and the whitest sneakers I ever saw jumped down, said goodbye and pushed the door shut with two hands.

She walked right up to me and said, "Hi! My name is Sara. I'm in Grade Two." I wasn't sure what to say. I must've told her my name. Sara was tall. She told me that the middle-schoolers and high schoolers were in the woods smoking and not to go there. They would come out when someone yelled "BUS!" We were to get on the bus first and to sit in the first five rows.

On the bus, she told me about the playground boundaries, and that I had the nice Grade One teacher. Albert, the bus driver, she said, passed out chips at Halloween, candy canes at Christmas, chocolate eggs at Easter, and Werther's Originals for no special occasion at all. Tuesday was the best day to buy lunch because it was pizza day. Vanessa was the Grade Two bully. She would tell people you peed your pants, make faces at you, call you names, and make rules like no tag backs when you were 'it.' Vanessa had a lot of friends. Anna was the Grade Three bully. She would push you and butt in front of you in the playground, but she didn't have as many friends as Vanessa.

I wasn't sure what a bully was, but I knew I was being warned.

Our bus, she added, was parked by the flagpole after school.

At recess I found Sara. She was at the Grade Two-er swings pushing some screaming girl up and up. Sara counted "Ten! Eleven! Twelve!" She turned her head at seventeen.

"Wanna push me? You get twenty-five pushes, then you have to switch," she said.

It was like asking. Do you want a pony?

I was in love with Sara. She was straight and tall. She was so clean, she shone. She knew everything and she wanted to talk to me! I soon learned that Vanessa and Anna did not mess with Sara. I wasn't sure why, but I think it had something to do with Sara being the tallest girl in grade two. On a rainy Tuesday, while we waited for pizza, Sara told me I was her best friend.

Sara is my first and only friend.

I remember busting the ice off the puddles the morning Sara didn't show up at the bus stop. They say animals can smell fear. Vanessa could smell the pheromones from across the hall. She told me that Sara was not around to protect me today, so not to bother going to the swings or the jungle gym, as none of the other girls liked me. Vanessa's posse raised their hands and voted me off the playground. At recess, I stood against the fence watching as one drab pigeon kept pushing another one with white feathers away each time it came too close to the group. I wondered where its friend was.

The next day Sara was at the bus stop. I was so happy to see her. I told her about Vanessa. All Sara said was she couldn't come to school yesterday because her mom was crying. Her dad was gone. He was not coming back. Her parents were getting divorced. I asked if her mom found out about special love and grabbing the stick. She didn't answer. Sara was going to stay with her mom.

Sara's mom was a nurse.

Sara grew into an athlete, the kind that has their name on the morning announcements no matter the season. Coaches wanted to coach Sara, teachers wanted to teach Sara and kids wanted to be Sara. I would go with her mom to watch her play basketball, volleyball, and soccer. People in the stands would talk about Sara like they all knew her, saying things like "Sara will be an NCAA Division I starter," "Sara needs better coaching," or "Sara is a winner." Still, we were best friends. The only thing we had in common was each other. I'm not sure why she never drifted away.

I remember waiting my turn at the Grade Eight district music festival. I saw Sara sitting with her mom. I couldn't figure out what they were doing. Then, after my recital, they were standing, talking my mom. When Sara said she missed basketball practice to come and hear me, it was like winning.

In Grade Seven, I had a plan to be so smart that they would skip me a year in school so I wouldn't be left alone in middle school with Jane. She was smart, pretty, and the leader of the Grade Seven social order. A glance from Jane and you might as well… well, it was like the kiss of death you see in the mob movies, except death would be a relief compared to the wrath of the girls. My average was 98.7. I won in the district science fair. My project's title: "Do graphite fly rods cast further than fiberglass rods?" I studied for the provincial math competition and came fourth when the winner probably never cracked a book.

I cried and waved through the bus window at Sara, who was waiting for the high school bus.

In Grade Eight, I disappeared. I would leave questions incomplete on my math tests so I wouldn't lead the class, because Jane liked to lead. If she ever started a campaign against me, I probably would've planned on leaving sooner. I took up the sax as a noon-hour activity. I studied for math competitions as a noon-hour activity. I learned chess, the only girl; another noon-hour activity. I would've been in drama, but Jane was all about the stage. People said I was task-driven, but really, I was just scared shitless.

I feel good about getting to tell Sara that I drove to school with Mr. Buckley, and that he stuffed the umbrella in a snowbank, bought me a coffee, swore and is a sax player too. And that I know about the Jag. It seems like such mature info and it's not gossip.

A tap on my sole. Sara.

I smile; I open my eyes.

7

Catching Up

I walk into math class. I update the list.

   √ Earrings
   √ Hug
   √ Supper plans
   √ Saxophone
   √ Library Books
   √ Clean out Locker
   √ Skip History/Money/ letter
      Lunch Sara/Lori
      Ice cream
      Mr. Frank
      Necklace
      Mail letter
      Supper
      Sara
      Breakfast Hug
      Pack Up
      Clean /laundry
      Leave

"Hey, ready for the test? I need to pass this – last term I made 50. I saw the mark on your last test. You're lucky. You've always been smart. This is all fuckin' Greek to me," Todd says as he slides into the seat behind me. "I wish I had your brains."

He doesn't usually sit behind me.

I push my list into my bag. Todd has been in my classes since elementary school. He's a drama guy. In middle school, he was Shrek. He talks to me like he knows me. Sara said he's too shy to ask me out, and I said I didn't really like him so she wouldn't meddle. I could like Todd, but how do you keep the line between friendship and sex?

I don't know if I could ever let a boy hold my hand, have him lean up against me, play with my hair or brush his hands over my breasts. To him it would be affection, excitement and anticipation. I could stroke his penis, spread my legs, or let him ride me like we were dogs, but I would be cheating him out of emotion that he might think is happening, when it would really be just a lot of heavy breathing, squirting and making a mess. I keep our relationship distant.

"You think if I come down where you sit in the morning, you could help me out a bit? I think I could pass if I could at least get the assignments done better," Todd says.

"Sure," I say, realizing I'm going to have to stop lying. I turn my head into my backpack and act like I'm looking for a pencil. I don't want to risk him getting over his shyness. Looking up, I accept a test from Mr. Smith.

"Thanks."

"You're welcome, and good morning, Darby."

A yawn comes over me as I circle B. The trig functions are easy. I can't see how Todd could fail this.

My head bobs, my neck catches it and bounces me back to math class. I read about angle of declination. My pencil slides a scribble across the page.

A salmon emerges from the water like an atomic sub surfacing from the ocean depths. As it smashes down on the surface, my reel starts to whine.

"The princess has one!" comes from across the pool.

He gets into my backing before I have time to get my rod up. It takes me ten minutes to retrieve him. Then he runs out the line again. I wade with him down the pool.

"Stay with him, Princess," says a man reeling his line in to let me pass.

The battle takes 30 minutes. One man old enough to be a grandfather wades out with two stones in a net, scoops up the silver torpedo.

"A ten pounder!" he yells as he walks the net toward me.

"Congratulations!" comes from behind me. I turn around and five men are standing on the shore.

"You're hooked! No turning back and at such a young age."

"It's half your size, Princess."

"Are you going to tag him?"

"No. I want to let him go please."

"Pictures first," comes from Dad. Snap.

The grandfather man holds the fish by the tail, head into the current and with a jerk of the tail he is back in the wild.

My shoulders are shaken and my head rubbed. "Congratulations… you're quite a girl… great fish…"

Moonlight floods over me; cool spring air tickles the tip of my nose. Crickets sing. My sleeping bag is being unzipped. I smell the gin. "I'm feeling so much love," he says.

His arms reach around me. I can feel the stick being rubbed up and down my back.

Tears roll down my face as his big hands squeeze my ribs. "I can't breathe, Dad." The slime runs over my back. Where am I going to wash up in the dark? My sleeping bag is a sticky mess.

A big fire in the morning. We burn my sleeping bag and nightgown. Dad rests his hand on my back as we watch the flames. The fire leaps up, and I watch the area between the flames and the calm.

"We'll tell Mom we forgot them if she asks, OK Darby?"

"Darby, Darby, Darby!" is punctuated with pats on my back. "Wake up, the bell's going to ring," Todd says.

My head spins back. I panic for a second. He leans away at the sight of my face. I twist back, then look down at a bunch of scribbles. I close my eyes, relieved that Todd doesn't know.

I see the waves of turbulence at the flames' tips and remember it was the first time I knew fully that the special love was not special. The 'love' took over the fishing, and the four wheeling, and the canoeing. Dad wouldn't talk after, sometimes for hours. He was always drinking. More and more undershirts and panties got ruined. He was starting to 'love' me when Mom was not at home. Skinny dipping was part of most trips even after my breasts became sensitive buds and my new pubic hair was dark red, and something I wanted to keep to myself. Rules about what to wear, what to do and where I could go, became part of keeping Dad happy. The lies about where we were, what kept us late, who was with us and the drinking, were piled on the special love.

I liked that I was the only girl in the salmon pool or on the ATV run. It was grown up to be driving the car, four-wheeler and snowmobile. Fishing was who I was. By age eleven I had fished with lawyers, judges, MLAs and million-aires, in salmon pools you needed to be invited to. I was Princess or Darby. I listened about politics, legal arguments, and brokered deals. The abuse was a collateral activity. Sara had a secret too; she wanted to be a doctor, not a basketball star. Basketball was her way of getting into a good school.

I started to help conceal the truth. I would pack extra underwear and clothes. I packed and unpacked for my trips. I did my own laundry in Grade Five. I was driving the truck home when Dad was too drunk. We would change drivers at the bus stop. I was twelve.

Once, Hank Peterson, a lawyer friend of Dad's, snuck into our cabin. Dad was in the lower salmon pool. I started my period and wanted a shower. I was singing *I Will Always Love You*. I felt cold air. I turned around. One hand was parting the curtain, pants to his knees, and with the other, he was pulling his erection. I screamed.

"Shh, I know your secret," he said, "but I won't tell, shh." He continued to masturbate in front of me.

I grabbed a towel, wrapped myself in it and rushed past him before the mess. I sat on the corner of the bed. I could hear Hank panting. How did he find out? Who else knows? A blue jay screeched. I checked out the window for Dad and worried that Hank might use the secret to blackmail Dad in Court. How mad Dad would be if he knew we were discovered! Hank walked past me and out the door. I kept my eyes on the cracks in the floorboards, then I went in the bathroom, got on my hands and knees and wiped up the mess.

That night, Hank came back to the cabin all smiles carrying a bottle of gin and a deck of cards. When the bottle was half gone, I announced I was going to the lodge for a snack. I got the sleeping bag out of the car and slept in the lodge on the couch. I knew Hank wouldn't give up.

"… OK, let's make sure our names are on the tests, as the bell is going to ring," Mr. Smith says as the bell sounds mid-sentence.

"Darby, you were out cold," Todd says as we walk up the aisle. "I would've woke you earlier but I didn't notice. You OK?"

I start to feel it. "Yes, I'm fine. I have to run, catch you later!"

I quicken my stride as if someone is waiting for me, and leave Todd in the flow of the hallway. I turn down the hall. I swallow it down. I rush into the bathroom. My mouth is full. I push through the stall and grab my hair, hold the door closed with my foot. Night dreams don't seem to bring it up, but dreams in school, at Sara's, in the daytime do. It's a race every time. I sit on the toilet, the bell goes, the warning bell. I bend over to look under and through the stalls. No feet, no legs, I come out.

8

Washing My Hands

I've decided to skip Mrs. Johnston's history class. I never liked her anyway and I've taken the class off before. She never checks because she doesn't like smart, dumb, beautiful, ugly, forceful or meek girls. If we are not there, she has all the boys to herself to patronize. Every girl in the school knows this.

Taking class off is easy. I started skipping last semester, about a period or two a week to catch up on homework, sleep, or to plan. I cut class right out in the open. It is easy if you have good marks and are never in trouble. The librarian just takes my word on 'Mrs. Johnston sent me down to do some research', because everyone knows Mrs. Johnston doesn't like girls, or if you have Mr. Cutter, you sit in the cafeteria and say to the V.P. 'Mr. Cutter said I could come down here and work', because every V.P. knows Mr. Cutter's class is a circus. For gym, I play the period card.

I walk into the library, find a seat in the back. Opening my textbook, I go to the computer and search French Resistance in WWII. Pull the books from the stacks, flop them open to random pages, pull out a duotang, pick the wires straight, get two sheets of loose-leaf.

Dear Madam

I read the story about your organization last Fall in the Sunday paper.

I would like to thank you for the effort you put forth in the community in trying to help girls and women who have

I take the roll of twenties and a brown bubble envelope from my backpack. I peel one from the roll and slide it down into my pocket. I place the twenties in three equal piles and flatten them under a book.

Hestia House
Saint John, N.B.
E2H 1P6

I paper clip the bills into piles. I place them into the envelope like they were contraband or a secret message being shipped across enemy lines. I peel off the sticky seal and close up the package. Then a smile. I would not make a very good secret agent. Slipping the envelope in my pack, I walk to the office.

"Yes, Darby, can I help you?" says the secretary, looking up over her monitor. Hearing my name makes my mind stop. I form a question.

"Yes. I was wondering if you had postage stamps and if you do, if I could please buy one?" I say, then I think maybe one is not enough. I don't want my parcel returned to the post office. Three would do it, I think.

"We do," she says slowly, "but we don't usually sell them. Just one?" Her voice is warm, so I decide to ask for three.

"No, I would really like three please."

"Would you like me to put your parcel in the outgoing mail?" she says as she passes me the stamps and I pass her a Toonie and a Loonie.

I'd already decided to use the mailbox at the bus stop. "No thanks, my parcel is in the library."

"OK then. Just a second and I'll get you some change." She walks back to her desk. I read her nameplate and I wonder how many times Mrs. Walsh has made this trip: desk, counter, desk, counter? I count her steps: seventeen. Fifty times a day, 850 steps, 4250 a week, 80750 a school year. Does anyone care? "There you go, dear. You have a nice day," she says as she drops the warm change in my hand.

I thank her and wish her a nice day too. I peel and press the stamps in place, put the package back into my pack, reshelve my books. I leave the library and turn into the bathroom. I want to wash my hands.

9

Thanks

"I was thinking of eating with Jessica, Rachelle and Lori," Sara says as she pays for her lunch.

I'm pleased, because this is exactly what I was going to suggest and now I don't have to. "Great!"

"We're playing Rothesay High tonight. You comin'? Mom's coming after work. Call her if you want. I think we're goin' to Steven's party afterwards. Hockey stud, Luc, wants Rachelle to come but she won't go if we won't."

I know 'we' refers to Sara, Jessica and Lori. My acceptance into the volleyball girls' lunch table is because of Sara. The mayor of Gotham City didn't cancel the town council meeting because Batman brought Robin. Even though no one gave a shit about what Robin thought or had to say.

I want to spend some time alone with Sara tonight. "I'm not sure," I reply. "Mom and I are making pizza for supper." Then I realize whether Sara goes to the party or not, she will go home to get party-ready. If I go to the game, I can go home with her mom and hang out while she does. "Yeah, I'll probably make it. Mom will drive me," I say as we twist, twirl and shimmy our way to the table.

The school holds 1200 students and the cafeteria sits 500; the gym sits us all. Sara and I share a seat cheek to cheek. My knees bump Lori's. She looks up, smiles a greeting. Last month Rachelle was going on about a lesbian couple that cuddles up by her locker. Lori found my eyes. Her stare made Rachelle's rant fade into the cafeteria roar. I wasn't sure what she was asking me, "*Am I one of them? Ask me?*

Please give me a sign of support? There is something different about you too?" All of a sudden, I was scared, embarrassed, and guilty, so I looked down. When I looked up again, Lori had a napkin. She wiped her mouth, then her eyes. Since then, I have thought about the stare while looking at stars, ceiling tiles, or blank pages. I wanted to ask her, but I wasn't sure if she knew there was something different about me. I had already finalized my date so I didn't want to start something I couldn't finish. Then one night while I was lying on my bed and thinking of who Sara would have as a next-best friend, I thought of Lori.

"Sara told me about Mr. Buckley driving you to school," Lori says. "And you went out for coffee?"

"Not really," I say. This is the first time I ever knew Sara to tell anything I've told her. I swallow and shift upright.

"Joey is going to the liquor store after school. We should decide what it is we want. So, are we going or what?" Rachelle says, lowering her head and voice like this is a novel idea, four high school girls going to get liquor to go to a party.

Rachelle is in Grade Eleven and the prettiest at the table. Her cheerleader body wears a volleyball uniform. She is the only person I know that Sara is intimidated by. Sara has had no high school boyfriend, but I know she wants one. Sara told me that Rachelle has been on the Pill since Grade Nine and wants to start having sex. I think she thinks Luc is the man. I want to tell her that having a dick pushed up inside you is an intrusive mess. It lasts as long as opening a Christmas present, and you're left saying thank you for something you didn't like. There is no orgasm. Rachelle will always be looking for something that isn't there.

There is a silence, as it's decision time. I never go to parties, or drink, except at Christmas and the one time I took the Beefeater bottle out of the ATV saddle bag, twisted off the cap and tipped the bottle up. The gin felt cold against my lips. The smell of perfume filled my nose. I opened my mouth to let the cool clear smell pass through. My mouth burned. I coughed, but held my lips closed. I shook my head. I swallowed. It burned to my stomach. Every time I saw Dad's Adam's apple bouncing with the glug glug of air bubbles in the bottle, I thought the burning must painful. I felt sorry for him.

"I'm going, but I'm not drinking," Lori says, looking up.

"Let's get Coolers," Jessica says. "We got them last time. At least then you know what you're drinking. Last party fucking Ben kept trying to pour margaritas into me, acting like he was Jimmy Buffet. They got Samantha so drunk on them she passed out in the bathtub. Then Ben, Nathan, and Steven pissed all over her. I showered her off with her clothes still on, stripped her and had to dress her in Ben's mother's sweats. She kept saying I love you Jess, I love you, Jess. On the way home I told her mom she threw up on herself." Jessica shakes her head. "Samantha is such a stupid shit. She can't drink and she is going to get more than pissed on if she doesn't smarten the fuck up."

Jessica is big, and square. She's not pretty, but she's not ugly. We should all be as lucky as Samantha is to have Jessica find us when we need help.

"That Steven is such a fuck; it's a wonder he didn't pull his dick out and jerk off on her," Sara says. "Jenny thinks he's a stud. I think it's the only reason he has parties, so he can paw drunk girls. I got eight bucks. I'll go in on some Coolers," Sara says, as she hands over her five-dollar bill and change.

"Good, we'll buy twelve," Jessica says.

Dad never gets me drunk, but maybe he was Steven in high school. Maybe if I was drunk, the embarrassment wouldn't bother me as much. Samantha walks the halls like nothing happened, but everyone knows. If you're drunk, is it still your fault? Does anyone care after the embarrassment is out in the open? I'm sure that no one on the team has brought it up to her.

"You want to come, Darby?" Lori raises her voice above the hushed tones of the table. "It'll be fun."

Sara looks at me. "You want to?"

This is not the first invitation to tag along. I can't risk any foul ups. "I don't think so." It's the usual answer which is usually accepted.

"You sure?" Lori asks.

"I'm sure." I get up and say, "I'll be right back." I walk to the vending machine, pull my twenty from my jeans and press and collect change until I have five ice-cream bars. I walk back to the table of four girls wondering how many secrets they keep from each other. I know Lori has one.

"This is to put some summer in a miserable cold winter day." All four look up. I pass out the frozen treats. There's a round of "Thanks." No one asks why. If Sara wasn't my friend, I'd be eating lunch against my locker, on the floor, and they know but have never brought it up.

I smile *it will be OK* to Lori.

She smiles *thanks* back.

"OK then, we're a dollar twenty-five short," Rachelle says as she punches calculator keys. Stupid bitch!

I reach back down into my jeans and get the change – a Loonie, two quarters and a nickel. "This'll cover it," I say. Beauty will get her what she wants.

"Perfect," Rachelle says.

"Darby, you sure you don't want to come?" Lori asks, juggling a mouthful of ice cream, frowning and rubbing her forehead.

The table laughs.

"I'm sure."

10

Frank Writing

Mr. Frank will be in his class because he is *always* in his class. He has a lunch club of sorts. These six girls eat lunch in his room every day. YouTube videos are played, karaoke is sung, and shrills randomly fill the air. Mr. Frank just sits at his desk and comes and goes, as he tries to organize himself. He is my favorite teacher of all time. In Grade Nine he taught me math.

He is my opposite. He can't find his glasses even though he has three pairs. He makes careless mistakes in his math, but he doesn't care because he knows someone will correct them, and the process is what counts. He forgets names but knows you. He talks loud, laughs and every day is a beautiful day. He starts every class with a minute of meditation.

One day I was staring at a math test and he got down on his knees beside me. He gently plucked the idle pencil out of my hand. I sat in stunned silence. He was so close I could smell fabric softener off of the crisp ironed shirt he always wore. On my paper he wrote:

Darby, you have a beautiful math mind. It is a plea-sure having you as a student. Thanks for paying attention in class and correcting my mistakes.

This last week it appears you are not the same happy girl that I have come to know in my class. I am not sure, but it appears sadness has entered your life. Your well-being is very important because if you are not happy it

is going to be difficult for you to cure cancer, play in the symphony, help send a human to Mars and keep an eye on my mistakes. We are at our best when we are happy.

If there is something or some way I can help make your life better please ask. We have a whole bunch of counsellors here, all wanting to help, but you have to ask.

Mr. Frank

Forget about the test.

I was shocked! My period didn't come. How did he know? How could he tell? My head went light and my toast rose from my stomach. I was going to woof all over him. I swallowed the vomit back down. Bile burned as it rolled over my throat. I took the pencil.

Thanks, I'm fine.

He knew I was lying. I kept the note. It was in my room between pages 133 and 134 of *Harry Potter and the Philosopher's Stone.* Last week I burnt it.

I walk into room 133. A girl is playing a guitar; three others pass me on their way out. Mr. Frank is facing the board. I stop a few feet behind him. I wait but he keeps on writing.

"Mr. Frank."

He stops. "Let me guess… Darby Saunders," he says, before turning around. The bell goes. The classroom behind me starts filling up.

"Wow, look at you, so tall and Grade-Ten-ish! I peeked into the jazz band practice last week for a listen. You were walkin' that dog around the room girl!"

Nothing but a small smile out of my mouth.

"How is life, and math going?"

"Good." Chairs scrape across the floor behind me.

"I was wishing for a day off this morning," he says.

"So was I." The second bell goes, signifying the start of classes.

"But for every stroke of bad luck comes good fortune as now I have the pleasure of you stopping in to see me," he says, reaching in his desk drawer. His eyes stay with me. I hold his stare. His right hand fumbles in the desk. I know what he's doing. I swallow like Pavlov's dog. He passes me a Werther's and twirls one open for himself.

"I don't think this visit is about math tutoring, or improvising sax solos." The room behind us is a low rumble of mumbles.

"Actually, I just came in to say hi, and tell you that I miss your class."

"Thank you. I figure after one year in Grade Nine with me, the math department has three years to clean up my messes. So, they keep me down here. You taking advanced math this semester?"

"Yes."

"Making ninety-something?"

"Yes."

"Well don't let the math get in the way of all the important stuff, like playing that sax at the coffee house next week."

"I won't," I say. The class has become almost silent as the music has ended. I remember last year, waiting in class while Mr. Frank finished conversations with visiting students, wondering what was being said, and somehow knowing that we were not to interrupt. I think we would've waited the whole period.

He reaches for a sticky note and scribbles his signature. This is the unofficial tardy slip of Kennebecasis High, questioned by no teacher.

I want to say, "I loved you," but bringing the words out in the open would cause him concern. I don't want to cause any chaos.

"You have a nice day, Darby."

"I will, Mr. Frank." He passes me the note. "Thanks for the candy."

"Thanks for the visit; you're the girl."

11

Giving Back

The locker room is abuzz with the weekend coming up. The PA blares about the volleyball game tonight. Dan has the locker beside me and is talking about going skiing at Poley Mountain. I slide my physics textbook in between my math and history texts. My backpack feels slack on my shoulder, holding gym clothes, a calculator, pencils, pens and my letter. I have gym class last period; it's an invitation to skip and consistently the same five do and another random five or six join them. I slam the door, lock it up for the last time.

I speed up my pace to make sure I intercept Sara on her way back from gym. Turning the corner into the wing, her ponytail swings in stride. I keep watching as she talks to Lori. I breathe in a few breaths and slow my feet. I have practiced this meeting a hundred times. We are just twenty feet apart, but she hasn't looked up yet. I move over so our paths will collide. I realize I am hot and probably sweating. She looks towards me.

"Hey, 'sup?"

"Hey," I say. I set my knapsack between my legs and reach behind my neck. "Sara, will you hold this for me? I forgot to take it off at my locker and I don't wear it in gym class." I reach out my closed fist. Sara stretches out her open palm. I spread my fingers and the gold chain clings to my hot, humid palm, but Sara's fingers close and she has it. My chest goes down, my shoulders drop and I stare at a loop of chain hanging between Sara's fingers.

"Sure," Sara says, then passes her gym bag to Lori. I watch as she drapes the chain around her neck; her eyes look down as she secures the clasp. She spins the chain around and lifts her ponytail. The gold lays down around the bones that hollow out her throat. Better than I planned.

"I won't lose it there," she says.

"I'll call your mom and I'll see you at the game. Good luck, Lori." I get a smile.

"We gotta run," Lori says. "Are you sure you don't want to come tonight? I'm not drinking."

"I'm sure," I say, and I continue on down the hallway knowing Sara will have a piece of me touching her, forever.

12

Being Cold

My head vibrates against the window, as the bus rolls and rocks along the river road. The rain has turned the Kennebecasis into a sheet of grey ice. I remember the idea of submerging myself in the river, and wonder if the mystery would ever have been solved.

I feel someone sliding into the seat behind me. "Hey." I turn around. It's Todd. "I'm sorry about not waking you up in class today. But listen, I am serious about getting the math help." His face goes slack; his voice quavers. "So… would you help me?"

"Are you sure you flunked that? Wait till you get it back. If it is that bad – yeah, I guess so." I turn around. I hear him move. I know he's not that dumb. In class, his pencil is always moving and he is always punching keys. Maybe he forgot I've known him since Grade One.

Suddenly, he's standing in the aisle. Plunk. He's beside me. I look over. He stares over the seat. I feel heat on my cheeks. He planned this. "I might not've failed it, but I need help… Hey, goin' to Steve's party? Jessica and Rachelle, they wouldn't shut up about it last period. I see you eating lunch with them. There'll be a hundred people there. The last one was big, but this one is gonna be da bomb. The cops are gonna have to shut it down for sure."

"No, don't really do parties," I say.

"No? You doin' the volleyball game? I know you and Sara are tight. Where is she anyways?"

"She always stays after on game night." I reach between my legs and pull my backpack onto my knees.

"It's Rothesay. It'll be packed. A bunch of us are goin' before the party."

"I'm not sure." The bus turns and gears down to climb the Fox Farm hill; three more minutes.

"I got a part in the musical. You still playin' the piano? I saw you in the jazz band during the Variety Show. Fuck, you can play." The bus stops. Todd stands.

I grab the back of the seat and squeeze past. I realize the boy in my space wants nothing more than for me to like him. Boy likes girl. I look down into the face of the disappointed. "Maybe I'll see you at the game." I start up the aisle. I should never have said that.

"See ya there," he says.

Albert passes me a Chocolate Kiss. "Happy Friday!"

"Thanks, Albert. Have a great weekend." I pause as Alyssa makes her way down the last step. I glance back. Todd turns away, hoping I didn't notice him looking. I wish I could tell Sara.

"See ya Monday, Darby." I pause again on the sidewalk. The door clunks shut, and the bus works its way uphill. With one foot in the snowbank, I swing my backpack off my shoulder. I pull open the mailbox and shove my parcel through. Thunk. I wait for a car to pass. I wonder how long Todd's been planning this.

I walk alone up Beauvista. What the rain started, the February sun finished, rinsing the roads to shiny blacktop, which feels easy on my eyes. A horn toot-toots as a blue Corolla passes. I smile and wave.

13

Re-Patriate

The umbrella is gone. I wonder if Mr. Buckley noticed.

I turn my head towards the Buckley's driveway. Two cars have crossed through the snowplow's wake. My eyes follow one set into the garage. The Corolla's tracks have crossed over another set, so the Jag was home first.

I go through our garage to check. The umbrella leans up against the garbage cans. Fuck, there's going to be a scene.

14

The Last Supper

√ Earrings
√   Hug
√ Supper plans
√ Saxophone
√ Clean out Locker
√ Library Books
√ Skip History/Money/Write letter
√ Lunch with Sara/Lori
√ Ice cream
√ Mr. Frank
√ Necklace
√ Mail letter
    Supper
    Sara
    Lori
    Clean/Laundry
    Breakfast hug

I leave the door to my bedroom open as far as the second plank on the floor. My eyes go to the bed. I look around. My dresser is perfect. The hangers in the closet are still spaced. Someone had been visiting my room. Last Tuesday the telescope was adjusted and there were wrinkles left on my bed. I close my drawers and then pull them back from the jam just a hair. I found the bottom two pushed tight. Then I see it, a blank space on my closet floor – my leather boots are missing. Sara calls them 'Mama Leave Them on Boots.'

It's Mom, but it wasn't her last Tuesday. I cross the hall to the bathroom, run some water and wash my face clear of evidence. I flop on the bed. It's probably Davey. Why?

The garage door motor clicks on. She's early. The garage door lowers. The door opens.

Clunk, clunk, clunk, clunk. My boots walk into the kitchen. Two grocery bags are set on the counter.

Clunk, clunk, clunk, clunk. My boots walk back to the garage. The door closes.

Silence.

The closet door opens…closes.

Sock feet walk back.

The fridge opens. Glass hits glass.

Upstairs to her room.

Flush.

Water runs through the drains.

Back down the stairs.

I get up, smooth my bed, go into the bathroom and wash my hands.

"Darby, honey! Are you down there?"

"Yeah, I'm coming up." I look up at the ceiling tile before climbing the stairs.

"How was your day, sweetheart?" I get a kiss on the forehead. Mom has changed into her jeans and a t-shirt. Her hair is pulled back, and she wears pheasant-hackle earrings. One time, Sara and I counted the looks she got on a trip to the market, the bank, and the hardware store. Sara counted eleven definite looks and twelve if you count the guy who let her have the parking spot at the hardware store. I wonder if Mom knows she's a MILF and if Dad knows how many men, as Sara would say, "check her out"?

"My day was great, Mom. I have been thinking about this pizza all day," I say as I rinse the mushrooms and green pepper. "How was yours?"

"Busy, busy. There were two funerals; both families were in – deciding, ordering, changing their minds, reordering." She takes a bottle of red wine from the bag. "Your father started the day off by throwing a fit about that stupid umbrella. You should've waited for the bus. Why didn't you come back? You must've been soaked by the time you got to Sara's."

I think of the drive and decide no.

"Well how was I supposed to know? The thing's probably twenty years old anyway. He'll forget about it as long as Davey wins tonight." Wine glasses chime behind me.

We work in silence. A routine we've had since I was six. I remember standing on the stool and dropping the salami and pepperoni slices, enjoying the slop sound as they made craters in the sauce. I graduated up to grating the cheese, then to using the sharp knife, then to pressing out the dough. Mom always makes the dough. I tried once to surprise her on the first Saturday she worked, but it didn't taste the same. Mom said it tasted great and what I wasn't tasting was her love.

"With all those funeral orders at the shop, does it make you think about your own?" I ask, keeping my eyes focused on the cutting board.

"Darby, that's a funny question to ask me!" Glug, glug, glug. She pours herself more wine. "Would you like this?"

I look over, take the glass and sip. I like how warm it feels. It tastes like Christmas. When I set my glass down, my fingerprints have ruined the perfect translucent sphere of glowing red light.

Mom is quiet for a moment.

"Yeah, it does I guess, in some ways. I think about you and Davey, hoping that at my funeral you still love me, but that you don't cry because you're thinking about times like this. I see you holding your children's hands, maybe listening to Alison Krauss singing *Down by The River*." Mom rolls the dough ball around the counter. "I'd like you and Davey to spread my ashes in the places where we've spent special times. I hope there are still some of those places not yet discovered," she says, patting and pressing the dough ball into a loaf.

I wipe my hands on a dish towel and reach for my glass, wondering why she didn't mention Dad. "Fundy Park, and Penobsquis Brook where we went fishing." My eyes try to catch hers but she is looking away. "My old room," I say, "where you used to brush my hair, and sang *The Pony Man*." Mom has stopped patting the dough, and there's a sniff.

"At my funeral," I say, "I don't want flowers because they die and waste away. I would pick *Hallelujah* by Kate Vogel." A melody fills my head. I begin as she always did, low and happy, and my mom starts to harmonize, but soon the phone rings.

I let Mom go to the phone, to change her mindset. She picks it up off the wall. Ring! She turns and smiles away a memory. Ring! Her left hand goes up and wipes her eyes. I didn't want to make her cry. Ring... Ring!

"Hello... this is Mrs. Saunders... yes, I'm Darby's mom..."

It's the school calling about me skipping classes, fuck! I'll say Sara's depressed, no, I'll just tell her Mrs. Johnston is a bitch. I push the knife into the salami roll, my eyes look at the board, my ears stay with Mom.

"She did. She never told me... we sort of just got in..."

Turning to her, I get the 'why didn't you tell me' look. It's Mr. Smith about the math test, shit. I'll tell her I couldn't sleep through the storm and I fell asleep.

"...well thanks. We think she is too."

Her voice lightens, a big smile comes across Mom's face, her eyes soften like they do just before she kisses tears away. Before I can mouth "Who is it?" Mom turns to rinse her hands.

"…Congratulations… I think she would do that for you…I think she'd love to. She is standing right here. I'll ask her… you don't have to do that."

Who is she talking to?

She puts her hand over the mouthpiece. "It's the neighbour, Mrs. Buckley. They just sold their house in Halifax and the buyer wants the deal closed. They want to leave for Halifax in an hour and want to know if you would dog-sit."

Dog sit, what does that mean? I have plans, but I have no plans for an excuse. I say, "OK."

"She said she'd love to… she'll be right over… bye."

"Well, sounds like you made quite an impression this morning, young lady," Mom says as she takes my wine glass and pours its remains into her own glass. "You better get your boots on and get over there. I'll finish this. Don't forget to brush your teeth, and there's gum in my purse."

15

Some People's Kids

Four hundred and seventy-three steps from our driveway to Mr. Buckley's. I pick my way up their driveway, keeping in a frozen tire track. I should've stayed out in the rain. How am I going to handle this? I spit out my gum; pull my hood down. Ring or knock? I knock.

A baritone bark beats me to my second knock.

"OK, Sasha!" I hear Mr. Buckley. Feet shuffle. The dog continues to announce that someone is at the door. Maybe I am her first house guest.

The knob turns, nothing happens, then a jerk breaks it free of the frosty jamb. "Come in, Darby," he says, holding onto a collar buried somewhere in the fur. "She won't jump on you, she's just excited. She knows something's going on and now we have company." The tail bangs off the wall. She manages to get her head up against my legs. I never realized how big she was. Her nose wedges between my legs, her head raises, almost lifting me.

I bend to one knee and we are head-to-head. I bury my hands into the hair behind her head and shake my hands like I'm shaking a birthday present. She wags and sways and her head goes down. "You're a pretty girl." I rub harder, she pushes back with her head, wanting more and nearly knocks me off balance. "She's bigger close up," I say. I stop, Sasha turns her head and runs off the landing.

"I can't thank you enough for doing this. It's a kinda last-minute thing and the buyer's lawyer wants it done tomorrow," Mr. Buckley says. "Please come in. I'll show you the lower level." I use my heel to pull my boot loose. I shake my foot free, first left, then right. We start down the stairs. Squeak, squeak, squeak. Sasha squeezes past, stops at the foot of stairs and looks back up, waiting. Squeak.

I pat the dog's head and then look up. "Here's the den. You can see we have a few boxes to empty. This is where Sasha sleeps at night." His hand rests on her kennel. "She has a dog bed upstairs as well, but she doesn't mind her kennel and if you're going to leave her here all night, put her in it. She'll go in, watch. Sasha kennel."

Squeak, her head tosses, juggling the yellow toy.

"Kennel up, girl."

Squeak. More head tossing.

I'm thinking: she's not stupid, you're packing, she thinks road trip. The kennel is not the car.

"Sasha, kennel." He reaches for her neck and gives her a tug. She drops a rubber hamburger and sulks in, turning to face the closing door. "Good girl."

We cross the hall. Mr. Buckley pushes the door open, reaches around for a light, click. "Our music room." Out of the darkness comes the shine of three saxophones on stands. One is silver, a Tanner. A keyboard sits to the left and an electronic drum kit is in the back. A lone Stratocaster sits in a stand. Laying on the couch with its neck up on the arm, is an acoustic guitar, a Gibson. Cords hang from instruments, a mixing board and mics. They snake through stool legs and around music stands to speakers. The wall has photos – people's arms around each other, some with instruments, all with smiles. In one, a black man in a red fedora blows a trumpet, a tall long-haired man with wing-tip shoes plays a tenor, with Mr. Buckley on his alto; all are swinging to a rhythm. "That's from the Harvest Jazz and Blues a few years back. We were opening for Delbert McClinton." I pretend I don't know who that is. I turn my head to a small bar that runs along a wall with four chrome stools. The bar is covered with shakers, tambourines, and CDs.

"It's still a bit of a mess. I'm thinking of taking the bar out, so I can use the space for teaching," he says, stepping between the stands. "The recording stuff is still in boxes." He looks back like he's waiting for me to catch up. "Come on in; I'll show you my new sax."

My manners tell me to move forward, but my mind is undecided. Drive, humour, shaking hands, talk, compliments, coffee, holding the door, alone in the basement. Does he know? I step forward to a man cradling a sax.

"Tom! You'll have to show her that another time if we're going to be in Halifax by ten," comes from upstairs. Its feminine tone blows the tension out of my mind.

He glances toward the stairs, then sighs, shrugs his shoulders, and gestures with his hands as though saying 'What're you gonna do?' "I guess she's right. Listen, when I get back, I'll have you over some evening and we can lay down a few riffs and make a recording of you playing Tupelo Honey along with Mr. Morrison. You can use it as your first demo," he says.

My voice doesn't answer, because I won't be here and the invitation hangs in the air. He starts towards me. I step backwards out of the room, hoping my silence isn't an insult. I stand still so he can pass me and lead the way up the stairs. Instead of going up, he walks past and sets Sasha free. She scoops up the hamburger. Squeak, squeak! She stops in front of me as if to verify it's still me. I rub her head and my hand skims her back as she heads upstairs. I wait for Mr. Buckley to lead.

I climb the stairs towards his wife. I wipe my hands over my butt, scrape my teeth over my lower lip, push my hair back from my face, wishing I had touched it up. Sasha stands with her head hanging over the top step, as if making sure I am coming.

"Sasha, let her up the stairs. This is my wife, Sally," Tom says. "I'll leave the two of you for just a second."

Tall, maybe heels. Her head is down, her left hand moves a pen across a pad, raven black hair hides her face. Sasha runs behind the island. Walking up to the island, I decide to put my hands on the counter. Her blouse is crisp. It is open, exposing her throat, and her chest, but no cleavage. She looks up.

"And you must be Darby. A pleasure to meet you." She sets the pen down and smiles. "Thanks for doing this on such short notice. I hope we are not interfering too too much with your weekend. Tom said you and he had a bit of adventure this morning." Her face is framed by hair that wisps off her shoulders. Her black brows, lashes and hair are contrasted by soft white skin. I look into perfect glass-green eyes, like a taxidermist had placed them. I must have seen green eyes before, but I can't remember.

Say something.

"Yes, I guess we did." I am not sure what to divulge about the trip, so I leave it at that.

"Sasha, move," she says, trying to get out from behind the island. "Tom, why don't you take the dog out for a walk so she can have a pee, and let Darby and I talk without being interrupted. Sit down, Darby." My eyes turn to the kitchen table. I sit. Sasha puts her head on my lap and I rub her ears. "Tom! Darby can't listen to me."

"It's OK," I say.

"Tom, give us twenty minutes," she says.

Mr. Buckley turns the corner into the kitchen. "Sasha, where's your leash?" He has changed into jeans and a sweater. Sasha goes to him, leads him down the stairs, and Mrs. Buckley walks around the island. Her blouse tucks into a black pencil skirt that is clipped at her knees. Hose run down her legs to her toes, no heels. She sits adjacent to me. I can smell a soft baby powder scent as she sets down a list and a half-finished beer. The door closes.

16

The Boss

"Finally, peace. I wish that dog would become a dog and stop being a puppy," she says, tilting the glass. "It really is a pleasure to meet you, Darby. Tom, who was dying to meet you, has been dragging me outside to hear you play for weeks. *Tupelo Honey* and *Baker Street*. Beautiful playing." Her smile is genuine. "When he realized it was a young girl playing, he was quite surprised and a little disappointed – how was he going to share blues riffs with a teenage girl?" She rolls her glass in her fingers. "I'm wondering how a beautiful young girl like you knows the blues so well?" Her voice goes silent as she tilts the glass.

I am not sure if I'm being baited, if it's rhetorical or if I'm being complimented. "Thanks."

"You're welcome. I called your mom back. We would like you to spend as much time with the dog as you can. You can hang out here or take her to your house. She'll be alright alone at night, but you can stay over if you wish. Your mom said it's OK. But if she's alone in the house, she'll destroy stuff, so she has to be in the kennel if she's going to be by herself. She'll know we are gone and she'll be sulky."

This is not what I wanted to happen! Things are starting to get complicated. I blink, and look from her French manicure to her eyes. I verify they are green, as green as grass waving under the water in the flow of a brook.

"Usually, we just send her to a kennel, but we didn't get the call till three this afternoon, and the last time, she got kennel cough. Tom won't send her to one without visiting it anyway. So, we thought of you. We want to pay you," she says.

"That's not necessary, Mrs. Buckley."

"Yes, it is. Even though you may see this as a favour, we are asking you to give up your weekend plans. So does a hundred dollars sound fair?" she says, revealing two fifty-dollar bills from under a sheet of paper. "It would cost thirty dollars a day to kennel her, so we are getting a deal. Fair enough?"

Todd's plan comes to my mind. "It's no problem. You sure?"

"I wouldn't have it any other way, and I'm sure you can find something to spend it on." She pushes the paper toward me. "Here's a list of numbers, procedures and reminders," she says.

My eyes admire the backwards slant of her handwriting. I can feel her watching me as I scan the list.

"Simple enough?" she asks.

"Simple enough"

"Alright then"– her chair scrapes the floor – "I'll give you the tour. You already got the downstairs tour." We climb five stairs to the bedroom level. "Sasha is not allowed upstairs, by the way. OK, the bathroom," she says, indicated with her thumb. "And over there is the spare bedroom if you decide to sleep here. Towels are in the hall closet. The other room is full of boxes." As I turn to lead the way back to the kitchen, I realize I'm not asking any questions. "Eat and snack on whatever you like." She starts to walk to the patio door, stops and puts her feet into a pair of snow boots. "Just throw those boots on your feet for a second," she says as she slides open the glass door. Winter pushes in. I put my feet into Mr. Buckley's boots. My eyes go over the fence – our living-room light flicks off. I can see my bedroom window.

It is level with the top of the fence. It looks a lot closer from this angle.

"Damn it's cold," she says. "So, the hot tub." A beige circle is tucked into a rectangular cubby hole, hiding it from the neighbour's – our – view. "The temp is 101. I'll turn it up to 104 and it'll be toasty." She pulls the handle and the top tri-folds behind one end of the tub. "Here are the jet controls." The water whirls like a witch's cauldron and chlorine fills the air. "Just climb in, relax. Close it up. Turn the jets back down. Feel free to enjoy it. Sasha will just lie out here with you in the snow. The pool is for another day. Got it? Let's get in out of the cold."

The kitchen is warm, we sit back down. Cold air still clings to my cheeks.

"Can I get you anything? Coffee, tea, pop, glass of water?"

"I'm fine, Mrs. Buckley."

"OK then. I put twenty dollars on the counter in case you take the dog for walks and pass the Irving. Sasha knows they sell dog treats at the counter. And, you can keep the change if you promise never to call me Mrs. Buckley again; Sally or Sal, will be more neighbourly. Tom, well, he is always a teacher, so he'll be Mr. Buckley." She smiles, lines crease her cheeks; the smile softens, waiting.

"Fine, Sally." It makes her smile again. The name *so* doesn't match, and I smile at the thought of someone who looks more like a Samantha, Elizabeth, Carmel, or possibly a Rachelle, being plain Sally.

"Let me tell you, it's nice to hear a woman's voice for a change. Tom's brothers were here last week and they all have sons. Hockey blaring, dishes everywhere, bathrooms a mess. They said they came to help us move in." She gets up and starts digging in her purse on the counter. "We didn't force you to stand up some boy tonight, did we?" She stops, takes a pack of cigarettes out of her purse.

She *smokes*?

"No, no boyfriend," I say.

The lighter wheel scratches the flint.

Her cheeks concave, showing her cheekbones, then gently, like blowing a kiss, smoke trails up into the ceiling fan. Her eyes watch the smoke trail dissipate into turmoil. "Excuse me for a sec while I crack the door open. Do you smoke, Darby?"

"No," I say as I peek a look at the microwave. 5:16, I'm still OK. The pizza dough is rising and I can still meet Sara.

"Good. Don't start. It's a dirty, filthy habit. It drives Tom crazy. I wish I could quit. Tom says you are in Grade Ten. Besides your music, what else makes Darby happy?" she asks, as she reaches for an ashtray on the island.

"Well, I fish a lot, and read," I say, wishing I just left it at music.

"When I was a girl, I used to go fishing with my dad, but I was too girly to impale the worms," she says. "Not really my thing. What are you reading now?"

"I just finished *Kit's Law*," I say.

"I've read it. I try to read whatever Maritime authors the library features. It's about..." she closed her eyes... "a girl raising her mentally handicapped sister out in rural Newfoundland, and a sex scandal of sorts. Am I remembering correctly?" she says as she blows smoke.

"Yes, pretty much," I say. "Kit falls in love with a boy, who she discovers is her biological brother. Then she wants to have her tubes tied so she can marry him and not have children," I say.

"Think you could do that? Marry someone, but never have children?" She butts the half-smoked cigarette.

"I'm not sure. I've never really been in love. I like kids. I think that love would trump children," I say, wondering where that came from. "How about you, are you going to have children?" Why did I ask that!?

"I think so. If you'd asked me four years ago, I would have said no, but I've been around children a lot over the last four years. It's funny how we change," she says, getting up. "Have you read *Glass Castle*? It's set in the sixties and seventies," she says, walking down the stairs to the living room area, leaving me alone at the table. Am I supposed to follow? I listen, no voice. I look at the microwave, 5:23. Two beer bottles sit on the edge of the sink, a Bose music system on the counter. "Got it," I hear as she comes back up the stairs, then sets a red-jacketed book on the table. "It's a memoir about a young girl like Kit, and how she overcomes a really dysfunctional family. It's a great read if you like, you know, reality and the human spirit. Oh, and Sasha is a great snuggler when you have a book."

"Thanks," I say, flipping the book over, then over again. I place it on top of the list.

"I want you to do me one more thing. When Tom comes back with the dog, would you take her back out for a walk, or to your house for a half hour or so, so we can get out of here without her crying and whining and runnin' after us? I'll leave the key in the mailbox. Would you do that for me?"

"Sure. I'll take her over to see Mom." The door opens as if on cue.

"Take good care of her and enjoy the privacy of the house."

We get up. I walk around Sally and I feel her height tower over me. I turn for the stairs and she rotates behind me. Her hand is on my back, guiding my turn for the stairs. Her hand comes off my back; strands of my hair linger in her fingers as I step down. I want to turn, but I'm afraid of leaving a lasting image. "Thanks, Darby. See ya Sunday night."

"You guys have a nice trip, Sally," I say, looking towards the door, pretending Sasha has my attention. Sasha starts twisting, turning, wagging and banging into the wall as I come into view. "I'll take her over to my house to visit my mom," I say to Mr. Buckley, holding my hand out for the leash. Mr. Buckley nods, then hands me control and Sasha turns for the door. I slip my feet into my heavy Skidoo boots.

"Thanks again, Darby."

"No problem!"

The door closes behind me. I am out in the cold where I belong.

Minor Complications

The winter sky is jet black and Venus hangs on the western horizon. The winter air makes the stars appear brighter. I wonder if it's true or if it's just in my mind. Looking down, I see Sasha looking up at me.

"I want you to know I didn't plan on this, and I know now that I should've walked to Sara's this morning. You will have to deal with the consequences." Her face says, 'I don't care because right now I'm going for another walk.' I rub her head.

My feet crunch through the crusty snow. Sasha's don't make a sound. She has no idea where she's going. For all she knows, I could be her new owner. Mr. Buckley and Sally could never return from their trip. She is happy to leave her world. I will leave like her.

"Let's go surprise Mom."

Another Lie

I grab the towel hanging off Dad's golf bag.

"Sasha, sit. OK, then don't." I take her front paw and wipe her pads; there is no sense in causing any more shit. I stuff the towel down into the club shafts. It'll be spring before he finds it. I shake my feet out of my boots. Sasha looks at the door, tail swaying at full mast. I twist the knob and she pushes the door open. Air thick with the aroma of pizza covers me like a warm hug.

"How was it, dear?"

I let the leash go in response. Sasha giddy-ups towards the voice. I stop to hang up my coat and wait for the surprise.

"My God! Look at you. Such a beautiful girl. Such a beautiful girl. You're the size of a pony. Darby have you out for a walk?" I walk into the kitchen; Mom is down on her haunches. Sasha is on her back, mopping the floor with her tail as mom rubs her tummy. "You love that, don't you babes, love the tummy rub." Mom stops and Sasha's nails slip on the tiles as she scampers to her feet. "Let me see, do we have a treat for this girl?" Mom reaches into the cupboard and comes out with a box of Bacon Dippers. She shakes the box. "Treat for the girl." Sasha sits. Mom holds out her fist, a cracker enclosed; Sasha's nose presses against her fingers. "Easy, nice girl." Her hand opens and the treat is taken with a slop and a gulp. "That's a good girl. That's it 'til after supper." Mom looks up at me. "What's her name? How were the Buckleys?"

"Sasha. Fine, they're nice." I see the wine is half gone. Mom won't be driving me to the game. "I didn't know you liked dogs," I say, grabbing the leash before she starts exploring the living room.

"When I was a little girl, we had a Border Collie named Skipper. Grampy had him before I was born. He would always fetch the mail, and he was at the end of the driveway every day when I got off the bus. In junior high he would carry my math text book to the door. The sky was high and blue, the day Grampy was at the bus stop. I remember knowing something was wrong. I was in Grade Nine. They found him lying at peace on the front porch, in the same place he lay for ten years watching for squirrels to chase from the bird feeder. Oh, Darby, I cried so hard when we placed rocks over the grave. It was my first funeral." Mom stops and washes her hands, saying, "Let's see if that pizza is done." The oven door reveals two pies. The cheese is shiny with grease and the circumference is golden brown. "Done!"

"It's too bad Dad is allergic to them," I say.

"He told you that?" Mom says, hauling two pizza pans out of the oven.

"I'm pretty sure."

"Your father doesn't like dogs because he thinks they dirty the house up. I don't think he's allergic to them. Why don't you go into the living room and move all the stuff her tail might sweep onto the floor. I'll hold her," Mom says.

At the coffee table, I pick up the crystal dish that never has candy in it. Next to it, a picture of Davey and Dad posing in a hockey portrait. Placing both on the bookshelf, I wonder if, when I'm gone, Mom will know how many lies I've told.

"Pizza's ready."

Mom carves her pizza with a knife and a fork. I use my hands. Sasha lies on the floor beside my chair.

"I was thinking of starting to play my guitar again. It's up over the garage," Mom says.

"Davey loves to climb up there. He'll get it down tomorrow," I say.

Mom nods. "But what I was really thinking, was if I bought you one, we could sorta play some together."

"That would be nice," I say, knowing Dad will not allow it to happen, and I know Mom knows it too. He'll start by complaining about the cost – *she already plays the piano and the saxophone*. Then he'll start on about Mom wanting to work, and that now she wants to play guitar. If Mom doesn't catch on, one night down in my room he'll tell me to stop.

"I want to go over to Sara's to show her the dog, see how the game went. I'll stop at Buckley's on the way back, maybe watch some TV with Sasha." Which will allow me to avoid Dad.

"You be careful and keep her on the leash."

"I will. Thanks for the pizza. Love you."

"Have fun."

19

Thinking of Every Detail

√ Earrings
√ Hug
√ Supper plans
√ Saxophone
√ Library Books
√ Clean out Locker
√ Skip History/Money/ letter
√ Mail letter
√ Lunch with Sara/Lori
√ Ice cream
√ Mr. Frank
√ Necklace
√ Supper
   Talk to Sara
   Lori (Buckley's)
   Clean/Laundry
   Breakfast with Mom
   ~~Leave~~
   Buckley's - note about dog
   Feed dog & take to Sara
   Leave

I close my door on Sasha's nose. I place my telescope on top of my desk, move my sax stand into the corner, and my nightstand, reading light and alarm clock to the top of the dresser. Sasha proof. I crack the door seal and peek at

Sasha looking back at me. "You can come in, but you're not staying."

I flop down onto my bed, flat on my back. Sasha's resting her jaw on the bed; her eyebrows twitch. I roll over, away from her eyes. I wonder what she's doing. I roll back. She hasn't moved. More eyebrow twitching. I think of last night. Would she just lie beside me and twitch her eyes? Would she bark? Would she protect me? Did Dad think about these things when he said he was allergic to them? Probably... he thought about the room.

The red numbers say 7:00. Sara will be home.

"Let's go say goodbye to Sara," I say, swinging my legs over her head and onto the floor.

20

Saying Goodbye

"You stay here for a second," I say as I tie Sasha to the snow-blower in Sara's garage. I knock on the door as I walk in. I hear Mrs. Campbell in the kitchen. "HELLO!"

"Hello! Darby? I'm in here," comes from the kitchen.

I walk to Mrs. Campbell, who is still in scrubs. I smell Kentucky Fried Chicken. Mrs. Campbell is Sara, like I am my mother. It is as if the two of us received only one set of genes. She is lean, tall, and square in the shoulders. She jogs and goes to spin class. Sara says her mom is avoiding men, which Sara is not. She told Sara once that she was never sharing her love again. Sarah's Dad remarried when I was in Grade Two. Sara calls his new wife the Step-Witch or Bitch depending on her mood.

"Hi, Darby. You missed a great game. Sara's up in the shower."

"I was having dinner with my mom, and I sort of got a weekend job dog-sitting. I brought her over to show Sara."

"Where is she?"

"In the garage, tied to the snowblower. She's pretty big."

"She can't be that big. It's freezing out there. Go get her."

Sasha stands extending her leash fully towards the door. Her tail is swinging. Her front feet start to march as I untie the leash. "Now you be a good girl, or you'll be back out here." I turn to see Mrs. Campbell in the doorway.

"Yes, she's big! What's her name? She won't jump on me, will she?"

"Sasha. She hasn't jumped up so far," I say.

Mrs. Campbell rubs Sasha's head. "You are a big girl. Sara will want to keep you." She looks up at me. "Whose dog is it?"

"It's the Buckley's. They moved into the Murphy place, and they had to go back to Halifax for the weekend because they just sold their house there."

"Well, that's quite a dog."

"Can I take her up to Sara's room to surprise her?"

"Sure, if you can find any room amongst the mess in there."

"Thanks."

I take the steps two at a time. Passing the bathroom, I hear the screeching of the shower curtain. I push Sara's door open until it becomes lodged on something. The floor is covered in heaps of clothes, a book bag, and a gym bag. The closet door, that serves as a hanger, I don't think has ever been closed. The floor is a boneyard of shoes, sneakers, and boots. The double bed is really a single bed because one side is used as a staging area for 'can't decide' clothes, 'going to wear again' clothes, folded 'I'm going to wear them this week, no sense in putting them away' clothes, this week's pajamas, and a bear called Bear. The walls are covered with posters of athletes hanging in the air as they interact with a ball. The top of the dresser is mayhem – brushes, jewelry, trophies, makeup, and other stuff. My necklace rests over the back of a stuffed unicorn.

I take a sheer red scarf that hangs off the mirror and drape it over the unicorn's back. Her computer's on; ICQ is open. I take a peek. She's chatting with Lori.

I wonder if I can hide Sasha under a pile. I push her rump. "Down girl, down Sasha." We both hear the bathroom door, footsteps and "Oh my God! Where in hell did you get the dog? It's fuckin' huge." Sasha bends and wiggles to get her head in a position for more affection.

"He is a she and it's Mr. Buckley's. He and Sally, that's his wife, had to go to Halifax on short notice and they called to see if I'd dog sit; that's why I missed the game."

"Whoa! Her nose is cold." I look and see that Sasha has managed to get her nose under Sara's towel. "That's enough of that," Sara says. Sasha then becomes fascinated with Sara's bare legs.

Grabbing the collar, I yank her back. She resists the pull, and I yank again. "You be a good girl, or back in the garage."

"I'll get some clothes," Sara says. She drops the towel like the unveiling of a sculpture. She doesn't care that her breasts are nothing more than two protruding nipples. She told me once that they will stay perkier longer that way, and that if her nipples didn't have a mind of their own, she wouldn't even have to wear a bra.

"Pass me those blue panties and those jeans." I throw them with my free hand. Sara pulls on the panties and shimmies into the jeans. Pulls a bra off the dresser, puts on a white shirt she buttons up and tucks in. "Ready; did you wear your boots?"

"No, I never thought about them. If you want, we can walk over and get them."

"It's fine." Sara gets down on her knees with her hands stretched out in a yoga dog pose. "Let that beast go." The room turns into a wrestling match of Sara, Sasha, and laundry. Sara finally gets Sasha into the same submission move my mom used, the tummy rub. "I wish so much I had a dog. I gotta get a picture with her. Here–" Sara grabs her camera. For five minutes, it's Sasha shots: Sara with Sasha shots, Darby with Sasha shots. Sasha won't jump up on the bed for bed shots, so Sara picks her up and puts her on the bed, but she jumps back down. "I guess that's it. I can't wait to get these developed!" She plops down in her computer chair. "I gotta tell Lori about her!" Sara plunks herself beside the sagging bed. Sasha puts her head in my lap.

"Sara?"

"Yeah."

"I want to ask you something."

"Go ahead."

"We've been best friends since Grade One and I want to know why. I know why for me, but why for you? You have so many friends that you have more in common with. You're practically a celebrity. Why? Truth."

Sara stops. "What do ya mean? We just grew up best friends. I guess it's 'cause maybe we knew each other before we grew into the Sara the athlete, Darby the musician. Hell, now that I think about it, I don't ask you about choice of keys and you never say I think you should've been more aggressive in the key. You're the only friend that never talks about spikes, three pointers, assists, stats, and scholarships. We have no secrets. You know that I'm scared of Rachelle, I hate my stepmom, and tolerate my dad. Because you know I want to become a doctor, not a basketball star, you even help me with my math."

Ding from her computer. "I squeeze against Sara to read the screen. It's Lori."

"Bring her 2 the party!"

"Darby or the dog?"

"Both if they'll come."

"Mom is going to drive me over."

"Darby says Sasha is not allowed out past 10."

"See ya in a bit."

The typing stops.

"I think Lori's gay," I say.

"What?" Sara looks at me. "How do you know?"

I rub Sasha's ears. "Remember when that fuckin' Rachelle was ranting and raving about the lesbian couple who cuddle by her locker, like she was the fuckin' Mother Superior or something?" I play with Sasha's ear; she moans. "Lori looked at me. Her eyelashes were wet, like almost crying. And when Rachelle was done ranting, Lori looked at you, probably wanting you to tell the bitch to fuck off. Anyway, I know she knows I know and she wants me to ask her." I look over to Sara. Sara's face is blank. Her phone hums.

"Did you?"

"No, I want you to do it. You're the one she admires, you're her friend. If her being gay is OK with you, then I think it's more important than my opinion."

"How do I do that?"

"Tell her the story I just told you, except lie. Say you saw her looking at me and wiping her face, or just stand up to Rachelle. Sara, you're the leader, lead!" I say, wanting to take back my last word. "Promise me you'll do it." I feel my chin quiver. The phone rings. "You," I breathe in to steady my voice, "better answer your phone." I hope Sara didn't notice I was on the verge. Sara types off a message. I want to leave, but I need the promise confirmed.

"Are you, OK?"

"I'm fine. Just promise me you'll do it."

"OK, I'll do it, I promise. I wish you were coming with us."

"I couldn't anyway. I gotta get this dog her supper. Come on Sasha." I get up. The bed springs squeak. Sara gets up after me and I lead the way out.

In the kitchen, Mrs. Campbell is sitting at the counter picking at a few French fries.

"You want a piece of chicken, Darby?"

"No thanks. I gotta get going. Sasha, down girl. No chicken for you."

I look over at Sara. "Call me tomorrow, OK?"

"I will."

21

Out of Hell

Turning up Wiljac Street, I wonder if Dad is home now. I know he's going to throw a tantrum about the umbrella. He doesn't let anything go unpunished. I look up into the Drinking Gourd; Wiljac Street runs right into the North Star. I imagine all the slaves that followed that beacon into the night, leaving their hell and going somewhere, anywhere; even death was better. I jangle the leash. "C'mon Sasha girl!" I start running.

22

On the Trail

The mailbox squeaks a complaint as I lift the lid. My fingers brush over cold steel, feeling for the house key; my rising panic eases as my fingers finally find it, lying flat. I push it against the box's wall and flip it on its edge. I turn the key in the lock, bump my shoulder into the door. "There we go."

Sasha runs into the darkness before I can get the lights on. The house is eerily silent. I walk up into the kitchen, and on the table, I see the book, the list, and an envelope with my name on it.

"Let's get you fed," I say as I pick the chrome bowl up off the floor. Two scoops of dried kibble clang into the bowl. "There you go girl!" Sasha has her face in the bowl before I even put it down.

I look out the patio door and over the fence. Just Mom's bedroom light is on. She is probably reading. Picking up the book, list, and envelope, I turn off the lights and walk down into the living room. A woodstove is at the far end. At the base of a limestone chimney, a box of kindling and some firewood are piled into a round wood holder. The list didn't say anything about not making a fire and there are lots of ashes in the fireplace. I have made hundreds of them while camping.

I strike the match, and get the newspaper lit. I close the door, leaving it open a crack, letting the house feed the fire to life. I hear the first few crackles of the kindling and watch through glass as the fire gains strength and casts warm light around the living room. I get up, walk upstairs,

I look out the window and check Davey's room. It's still in darkness. I return to the fire and sit on the floor with my back against the couch.

Sasha, done eating, lies down beside me, her body leaning up against my outstretched legs. "There we go. We're just like those slaves hiding from their master on the journey," I say, rubbing Sasha's rump; her tail thumps against the floor until I stop.

I rip the envelope open, tilt the letter towards the fire; but the light is not strong enough for reading. I spy a small reading light at the other end of the couch. "Excuse me." I fish it behind the couch, pull the drapes, rest the light on the couch's arm and turn on its single bulb. I find my place by the fire; Sasha finds her place by me.

Darby,

Thanks again for doing this for us. It is very much appreciated. It was a pleasure talking to you. I am looking forward to your thoughts about Glass Castle when we get back!

Tom is really happy that you get along with Sasha so well. Thanks to you, I won't have to listen to him go on about the dog being in a kennel!

He wants you to know you are welcome to play the horns.

There are lots of snacks and stuff in the kitchen. With a little exploring I am sure you'll find them. Have a great weekend! Enjoy the privacy. Wrinkle your toes in the hot tub.

Isn't it funny how an inverted umbrella can lead us into relationships?

See ya Sunday!

Sally

I close the letter and fold it back into the envelope with the bills. "This is not going to change a thing, you know. I'm on a journey. You and your family have interrupted enough. I've given most of my life away today. Tomorrow I am leaving. Tomorrow morning, I am going to drop you off at Sara's. You'll be as happy with her as you are with me. I haven't figured out a lie to tell her yet, but it will come." I get up, part the curtains and look over the fence: both upstairs bathrooms are lit up. "Good, we can break camp in about an hour." I throw another log in the fire. The stove's fan comes on, blowing warm air into the room. Back on the floor, Sasha repositions her head so it rests on my thigh. Her head is heavy, and I feel the warmth of her back pressed against my legs. I crack the book. Sasha's breathing becomes heavy.

23

The Glass Castle, Me and Sally

Jeanette, the protagonist, lives in a completely dysfunctional family but she thinks it's normal until she gets to about age twelve. Then, she realizes she is a victim. Jeanette's problem is out in the open to everyone: she is poor, her dad is alcoholic, and her mom is bipolar. Jeanette does not have to explain.

My life appears normal to everyone, even Mom.

Does Sally guess something's wrong? Does the fact that I play sad songs to no one, have nothing to do on Friday night and no boyfriend mean something is odd?

"How does such a young girl know the blues so well?"

The fire is coals. My house is dark. The kitchen clock says 11:23.

24

Breaking Camp

I let Sasha out in the pool yard for her pee. I push my arms through coat sleeves and slide my feet into my boots. One big mellow bark comes from outside. I slide the door open and in she enters. "Did you know you bark in D minor?" I pick the snowballs off her legs. Sasha looks up at me and runs down to the landing and grabs her leash. It clatters on the stairs as she runs back up to me.

"No walk. It's bedtime. Come on." I head downstairs. I look up and she's looking down from the top step. C'mon Sasha. Kennel up." I walk back up the stairs, grab her collar. "C'mon girl." She comes down the stairs, her head drooping. "Kennel, girl." She looks up. I pull. She braces front paws down. I push. She walks in a circle. "OK, just a second." I run upstairs; she runs behind me. She stops at the door. I grab a dog treat from the closet. "Come on! Treats! Sit Sasha." She sits. I wave the treat. Her head follows my every move. I throw it in the kennel. Sasha looks up at me, her rump firm on the floor. "You're not that gullible, I guess." We look into each other's eyes, and I decide to do something I've always wanted to do. "OK then, I'll take you with me, but you have to promise, no barking, and you can't leave the room. OK?" As if she knows it was an invitation, she runs back up the stairs and we go out.

"Shh." We walk around to the back of my house. I step high to keep the snow out of my boots. "Shh." I look up at the dark windows. I brush the snow away from the basement walkout door. My stomach is full of butterfly and moth wings, my heart beats with the excitement of the mission. Sasha looks straight at a new-to-her door. The door opens easily, spilling some snow onto the cement floor. The room reeks of hockey gear hung up to dry. "Shh." I flick the light switch so as to not to risk tripping over a hockey skate. "Shh–quiet." Light off. I pull the next door open, revealing the downstairs hallway. Toes to heels to loosen my boots. I shake them off so I can keep my hand on the leash. I lose a sock. Ten steps to my room. I check the door before we go through.

"So far so good. Hey girl. Here's the plan. You get the floor. I'll give you a pillow," I say, warming my hands in her fur. "You've put me a little behind schedule, but I can clean this up tomorrow. Now it's bedtime."

I find a hanger for my coat; pull clean pajamas from the dresser. I set a pillow on the floor. "This is a lot better than a kennel." I scan the room for potential tail collisions. I wipe up the snow melt with my dirty pajamas. I slip into the warm flannel, between the sheets. Sasha sits with her head resting on the bed. The red numbers say 12:13.

I make the room dark. Sasha's body hits the floor. The stars are vivid. I smile thinking this is the first time I've gone to bed without brushing my teeth or washing my face. It's also the first time I've snuck in the house, and have an unapproved house guest.

Sasha sighs.

The water pump clicks on. Shit! "Shh!" I sit up, Sasha stands up and shakes her ears, a sound like wings flapping. I start stroking her head and the back of her neck. My heart is beating so loud Sasha must hear it. "Please Lord not tonight." I think about jumping out of bed, and going back to the fire next door, or just hiding in the basement. The pump clicks off. "Shh, good girl." The dishwasher opens and the glass rack rattles. It's too late to run. I listen for feet on the stairs. "Please, please, please…" My hand grips Sasha tighter. The muscles in her neck tense.

Should I get up, get dressed and pretend she is just visiting? I decide to stay put. My mind races for excuses… I'm sorry about the umbrella… She's just a dog… She wouldn't stop barking… I'll take her back; it will only be a minute… I have dog-sitting money to buy another one… I love you… I was waiting for you. "Shh." Silence creeps back, filling the void between my room and upstairs. I hear my breath run out of my chest. "You're a good girl. We've avoided the Master on the last night."

I pull the blankets up and my mind reaches for sleep.

25

Last Lesson

I make the final adjustment to my neck strap. Step closer to the microphone. A soft G floats from my horn and I work up the B-flat blues scale. Musicians with headphones on noodle away. I feel a body pressing up against mine.

"Let me show you another way to get the B flat." A hand reaches around from behind with black hair on the fingers and a gold wedding band slightly embedded into the skin. Fingers lift mine and move them over the pearls. The hand leaves mine and lingers on my breast, runs down over the curve of my hip. The musicians gawp.

A black man wearing a red fedora holds a trumpet and says, "If she is going to record with the band, she has to play with the band." There is a roll of laughter from the tenor in wing-tip shoes.

The pressure on my back pushes and grinds against me.
"Sally! Help me, Sally!"
Horns fill the air, drowning my voice.
"Sally! You knew!" I'm trying to move but a pelvis keeps rubbing up and down my back. "Sally, I thought you wanted to help."

I sit upright in the bed. My nightshirt is soaked. My heart pounds. Mr. Buckley is in my bed. I push him away and my hand touches Sasha's fur. I try to catch my breath as I reach across Sasha for the light. Was I yelling out loud? Sasha's head rises with the light. She looks at me like she must've been sleepwalking and somehow ended up in the bed. "You look innocent." The red numbers say 5:13. "That's it. No more nightmares for this girl." I take some deep breaths in through my nose, out my mouth. "Listen, I have to pee, so you have to be quiet." I slip my feet into the fleecy slippers that Sara gave me for Christmas. Sasha puts her head back onto the bed. I walk to the bathroom wondering how she knows I am coming back.

26

Final Adjustment

I adjust my pillow and sit up. I try to pull the blankets up, but Sasha's weight makes it impossible. Dad and Davey will be up in an hour to hit the road. It'll be easier to keep Sasha quiet if I'm awake. But if she barks, it won't make any difference – they'll have to leave anyway. It'll only be a few minutes of yelling. "Get that damn thing out of here! Joanne! Darby has a goddamn dog in her room! Can't you control that girl for even a day? It better be gone by the time we get back!"

"I'll run you to Sara's and tell her I promised my Mom I'd clean the house, and say if she'll keep you until lunch, I'll split the money with her." Since Sara loves money, especially money her mom doesn't know about, the white lie will work. Then I can come back, clean up and pack. I'll throw a load of laundry in before breakfast. Sasha rests her head across my thighs. "Don't worry about Sara, the wrestler. I'm sure you'll be allowed on the bed."

Sasha's head comes up, cocks towards the door.

"Shh." There's activity in the kitchen. I hear voices, but can't make out the conversation. I start stroking Sasha. "It's a man you don't need to know and a boy who would probably go bananas if he knew what I was hiding, shh." Davey starts down the stairs. Sasha gets up on her belly. "Shh just a boy going to hockey, Shh…" Davey goes past the door dragging his hockey bag.

Sasha looks towards it and back at me. "He's a good boy, shh," I say, stroking her neck.

An air of calm comes over me. It only takes a few minutes for the house to go quiet. The garage door didn't open, so they must've gone with the Millers. Not necessary for my plan, but convenient.

27

Pancakes and Sweetness

Smoke rises straight from chimneys as I scan the predawn horizon. Venus is still hanging on, but she will soon give in to the sun's strength. I place my feet in the frozen boot tracks from last night. My bare knees feel the bite of the winter chill.

"OK, go have a pee. Hurry girl." She bounces about ten feet in our tracks from last night, twirls and squats. Her head turns to the pool fence and we both look towards the sliding glass door. "They're not home." Shit! I'm in my housecoat and slippers; if she bolts, I'm screwed. "Come on girl, pancakes and syrup, yum, yum!" She shakes as if cleaning the stale air out of her coat and dog-trots back. "Good Sasha." I pat her head. "Let's go and make breakfast."

I strip the bed, and organize the second load.

I decide to get dressed so I can leave as soon as Mom does.

The eggs go puff puff into the flour. "Pancakes are my specialty. The secret is not to mix the batter too much. Mom likes hers thick and gooey in the middle. I like mine thin and crisp, with molasses. I'm sure you don't care, but don't tell you had homemade pancakes, 'cause it's not on the list."

"Darby, who are you talking to, dear?" comes from the top of the stairs.

"Sasha." I start the coffee. "I'm making pancakes, so don't be long."

Mom comes into the kitchen, wearing bad hair and her housecoat. "Wow, what did I do to deserve this?" A warm hand runs down across my back, then she turns to Sasha. "I didn't forget you! Morning gorgeous." She runs her hand down Sasha's back. "Have you been over there and back already?" she says as she reaches into the fridge.

"No, she spent the night in my bed."

"It's a good thing your father didn't find out. Last night he found dog hair on the kitchen floor, and I had to explain it was just a visit. He's not over the umbrella incident yet. I would suggest you vacuum. I'm going for a quick shower. Ten minutes, OK? And thanks." Her lips caress my cheek as I begin to stir the batter.

I remember the cook at Big Bend Lodge telling me that when spit hopped on the griddle, it was ready. I decide not and spoon on something better, butter. I hear the bathroom door open and ladle in the first two, wait for the bubbles, then flip.

"They smell great!" Mom says as she comes back into the kitchen, her hair wet, and reaches for plates. "Listen, your dad wants to go out to a birthday at one of the partners' tonight. It's a surprise for his wife. She is turning fifty. You know what he's like about office stuff. The team won both games yesterday. They're expecting to be in the finals tomorrow morning because they've already beaten one of the teams they're playing today. I wouldn't suggest having the dog over," she says.

"The Buckleys said I could stay over there, and Davey's twelve, he can stay by himself. He'll be tired anyway and he could just call me if there was a problem," I say, trying to come up with a solution that will ease her mind for the morning. Her brow furrows as she swipes molasses trails around her plate with a chunk of pancake speared on her fork.

"I suppose." I watch her push a chunk of pancake, making a path through maple syrup. "I just don't want another episode with your father. These pancakes are great. I have to get going. I'll be back at lunch," she says as she gets up.

"I'll clean up," I say. I pull my feet from under Sasha who is lying up against my shins.

"Thanks."

The last of the batter fills the pan. "Syrup or molasses for the girl? You have both colours in your fur, so why not both?" I plop a golden pancake on a plate and twirl designs with the molasses. The syrup just flows over. I take a knife and hack the pancake to pieces. I place the plate on the floor. "That's for being a good girl."

I start the cleanup by filling the sink. I hear the plate sliding across the floor, then up against the chair legs. I pick up the plate; it's clean as a whistle. I offer Sasha my plate; her pink tongue presses flat against it, pushing so hard I have to use two hands to resist. "Great stuff, got one more." I soak the dishes, I listen, I wipe the table, I straighten the chairs, I stack the placemats, I put away the coffee, I wipe up the machine, I listen, I wash the drips off the molasses container, I turn on the radio, I wipe up the stove, I wipe the fridge handle, I turn down the radio, I listen, I sweep the floor, I check the dishwasher, I listen, I hear Mom coming down the stairs. She stops at the foot of the stairs, fiddling with her earring. She wears the soft green sweater that she loves, perfect for this cold winter morning.

"You look great Mom, just great," I say.

She beams and her eyes soften.

"OK then, give me a hug." I wrap my arms around her and squeeze. I kiss her cheek and she kisses my forehead softly so she doesn't smudge. "Love you, honey."

"Love you too, Mom." A wave of contentment washes over me. She'll remember the pancakes cooked with love, that she kissed me goodbye and she'll never have to know anything else.

Drop Off

8:02. No sense in going to Sara's yet. I have lots of time.

Sasha lays in the middle of the floor as I finish the kitchen. She follows me back and forth from bedroom to bathroom to switch up loads, back upstairs for the vacuum hose, then downstairs dragging the hose. I run the vacuum up and down the hardwood planks on my floor. I follow the parallel lines to make sure I get it all. I get down on my knees to do under the bed. I feel warm saliva in my ear. "Yuck! Stop that you crazy thing!"

I push her away but her tongue attacks from another angle. I push her again but her sloppy onslaught continues. "I am not Sara!" I get to my feet. "You're having too much fun." I open the dryer and fluff up my sheets: twenty minutes left on the timer. I lug the hose upstairs.

It's 8:32. Sasha comes up behind me. "Are you afraid I'm going to sneak out of the house without you?" I run the vacuum over the ceramic tiles. I do four tiles then move to the next four to cover the floor. I can see Sasha's white fur being sucked up. Her black and brown hair is hidden away in the tiles' sandy brown. I continue down the hallway. "There. Done." I go back down to the basement for my boots and coat.

8:53. "Lots of time! Let's go see sleepy Sara."

We pass the Jeep and the two ATVs on our way through the garage. The ATVs have no catalytic converters, so they'll produce enough on their own. I'm happy that I'll be able to lie down in the back seat of the Jeep.

The sky is blue. The gusty wind ruffles Sasha's fur. We make the turn into her driveway. "Let's hurry!" I kick off my boots on the landing. I leave my coat on. We find our way to the kitchen and dump the kibble.

I find last night's note and flip it over.

Sally,

I'm sorry I had to leave, but the trip was planned so long ago I couldn't change my plans and I didn't want to ruin your trip.

Last night Sasha and I read by the fire. She is a great cuddler. She did not want to get in her kennel last night, Friday, so she slept at my house with me. She is currently with Sara Campbell, 134 Fox Street, 567-4576. Sara has already met Sasha and they will be fine together. I gave fifty dollars to Sara.

It was a pleasure meeting both you and Mr. Buckley.
Darby

I slide the seventy dollars back in the envelope, and put the list on the table. Sasha slurps water out of her dish; she looks up, dripping. "Time to go for another walk. I have a schedule to keep." The microwave says 9:22. I'll be home by ten easy; two and a half hours.

I break into a run, and the two of us are running onto Fox Street. Sara's car isn't in the driveway; her mom must be working. I reach up into the frozen dead leaves of the hanging basket to retrieve the key.

I wipe Sasha's paws on the mat. The house is quiet. A list is on the counter.

Sara,
Be home at 4:00.
Clean your room.

Switch the loads.
If you want your jeans for next week, wash them with your uniform.
Turn the slowcooker on at noon. I have set the temp.
Have a nice day.
I love you.
Mom

"Let's get her up! She has things to do." We head upstairs. I push the door open. Sara's dead to the world. Sasha's nose starts investigating between the sheets. "Come on, party girl," I say. No response.

Sasha's nose hits skin. Sara bolts upright. "Holy shit, what the hell's going on?" I sit on the edge and pat the bed. Sasha puts her front paws up causing the bed to tilt.

"Come on, princess, your wrestling partner is back. Time to get up," I say. "I need a favour."

"But I don't want to go to school," Sara says as a small smile crosses her face, and her hand reaches out to rub ears.

Sasha jumps down off the bed as the door across the hall opens. My eyes follow her.

"Wow, is that your dog, Darby?" Lori's standing in the doorway in a T-shirt and panties. She uses two hands to ward off the nose.

"No, I'm dog-sitting," I say, and don't know if I should ask a question in return, or make a statement.

"We had to walk back from the party," Sara says. "Our drive got so drunk Lori wouldn't get in the car, which I have to say was probably the right decision, so we trekked it here." Sara sits up, and Lori joins us on the bed.

"How was it?" I ask. I pull Sasha's collar. "Leave Lori alone."

"It's fine. I have a dog," Lori says, as she rubs her hands up and down Sasha's neck. Sasha moans. "Let me tell ya, it lived up to its billing, with sex, drugs, fights and rock and roll. Steven was, as suspected, pissed, and there were lots of others, including our drive. They had a bong set up on the coffee table. The floor was so fucking slopped up, we left our boots on. What a mess! I don't know how he'll ever get it cleaned up and get the dope smell outta the house by Monday. And oh yeah, Sara has a new crush! Barry was flirting with her, offering her a line." Sasha butts against her leg. "Oh, you're such a nice dog." Lori picks up the pace of the massage; the tail swings in time.

"Oh, fuck off! More like trying to score a sale and a fuck," Sara says. "Oh yeah Darby, Todd was lookin' for ya at the game. He wanted to know why you weren't there."

"Some guys from Rothesay showed up." Lori says. "Next thing you know, there's shouting outside and the house emptied, so we decided to leave. Rachelle was attached to Luke, so we left without her. I don't know why she wanted us to go to the party with her anyway.

"Like I said, Jared was too drunk to be driving, so we started walking. When we got to the Irving, the cop car passed us, probably on their way to break it up. By the time we got here, we were froze. Sara made some hot chocolate. And guess what?"

I turn my head to face Sara. I don't want to get tied up in any more of Lori and Sara's adventures, or conversations from last night. I did what I had to do. I just want to leave. Sara gives me a quick glance and looks past me to Lori.

"What?" Sara asks.

"Today's my birthday," Lori says. "And I want to take you both out to brunch. Then maybe go see *Titanic* because I can't think of two better people to be with today."

Shit. I have to get this conversation back to my agenda. "Listen, Sara, I promised my mom I would clean my room, because the dog stayed there last night and Dad had a fit about the dog hair, so I have to vacuum. I wanted you to watch Sasha for me," I say.

"Darby, I've seen your room. It should take twenty minutes."

"I'll go with you," Lori says. "We can leave the dog here. It will only take ten."

"I have to watch the dog," I say.

"My mom is dog crazy. She'll take her with our dog to the bark park, while we eat. I know she will," Lori says.

"Yeah, but I can't go to the movie. I promised the Buckley's," I say, wishing I'd just locked the dog in the house.

"OK then, forget the movie. We can rent a couple, buy some junk food and watch them here. Or we can go sliding at the park. We can take the dogs," Lori says. "It's my birthday, Darby, and you're always standing us up. Today you're coming."

"…but Sara has a big list her mom left her," I say, grasping for support. I look at Sara, trying to hide the fear that's threatening to overwhelm me. My heart's beating into my neck. I turn my face towards Sasha. My chin quivers. I bury my sweaty palms in her coat.

"I never do it anyway," Sara says. Her expression changes. "Are you OK?"

"Yes. I never planned for any of this," I say.

"We're only going to Bacon and Yolks, and renting a movie," Sara says.

"Great! Let's get started," Lori says. "I'm going to get dressed."

"I'm going to the bathroom," I say, then get up off the bed.

29

In the Shitter

I push my pants down, lift the toilet seat cover. I sit on the cold rim. My whole life has been a series of well-told lies, manipulation, and sins. All I want is to leave today. I feel silent tears rolling down my cheeks. Why is this fucking happening? I grab some toilet paper. What am I going to do? They're probably talking about me. I know they are. Sara's going to know something is wrong. I have to leave; I have given so much away already. I wipe my eyes. That fucking dog! Should I just say no, go home and put the dog in the kennel? I can't leave with Sara being upset with me. It was so perfect last night.

I flush and pull up my pants, then turn on the taps and let the water run cold.

I think maybe tonight, or tomorrow morning when Mom goes to church. I'm going to have to stay at the Buckley's because Dad's going to come home drunk, and Mom tipsy, and I promised myself Thursday was the last time. In the mirror I see a girl crying. She's not sad. She's just crying. There's a welling in my stomach. I turn, drop to my knees. Pancakes and molasses splash into the toilet. I flush. My stomach heaves again, but I'm empty.

I splash water onto my face to wash away the tear trails and try to cool myself. I cup my hands in the flow to rinse the shit out of my mouth. I'm in a cold sweat. I pull at my clothes to loosen them from my sticky skin. I settle my mind on tomorrow morning, or Monday morning. I'll leave for school and just come back after Mom leaves. I'll just keep avoiding him. I spit.

30

Getting On With It

"Ready?" Lori says as I come out of the bathroom.

"Yeah. Let's forget my house; I'll get it after. This place needs a little more effort. How about I go down and switch the loads, and why don't you two gather up a few loads from in here," I say.

Sara stands in a pair of sweats tossing a tennis ball up and down. "Sasha want the ball? Want the ball?" Sasha's head goes up, down and around following the ball. The ball flies out the bedroom door, off the wall and down the stairs. Sasha barrels after it. I head down to the laundry room. Sasha, coming up, avoids my eyes so I block her path.

"Give me the ball!" I pull, but the ball is wedged in her canines. "Drop the ball girl." I tug, she tugs. I take my free hand and put it over her snout and squeeze my fingers and thumb, pushing her lips up against her teeth. "Give me the ball girl." Her grip loosens and I take the slimy ball from her teeth. "Ha! See that's the difference in evolution. I read *Field Dogs* while waiting for the fish to fry. Dogs sleep! Come on. I have the ball and Sara will get nothing done if you go back up."

The dryer is still warm; the washer is done. I pull dry clothes into the basket and pile the wet ones in, turn the dial to "45" and press start. There's an easy load of Mrs. Campbell's scrubs, so I stuff them in, pour in the bleach and get it going. "Those two are probably catching up on last night's romances, conquests, breakups, upchucks, pass-outs, fights, and arrests, and not getting a thing done. We'll stay down here." I start folding the load. "It'll be safer. Besides you're too much of a distraction. Don't worry, they haven't ruined my plan."

Sara enters carrying a mountain of clothes and sheets. "Lori's as bad as you," she says. "She called her mom. She'll be here in about ten minutes."

"These are done," I say, passing her the basket. "You can switch the loads when you get back."

31

In the Backseat

Lori's mom stands in the driveway with the tailgate up. She's bundled in her winter coat and snow pants, a toque pulled down over her ears. Her boots look like tiny mukluks. She is short; Lori is so tall. Her face is lined like a grandmother. "Good morning. Up early today girls." Sasha is already getting a rough rub down from Lori's mom's black leather mitts. "What's your name, beautiful?"

"Sasha," I tell her. "I'm dog-sitting for the weekend." There's a rattle of steel in the back of the hatch. A black lab standing in a kennel barks. *Let me out, out, out.*

"It's OK, Pepper. Sasha's going to the park with us. You can get acquainted there." Lori's mom turns to me. "No worries. He gets along great with dogs. He just thinks he's missing out on a little attention," she says. "Up in the car, Sasha. Let's go for a drive." Lori's mom pats the floor of the hatch. Up Sasha jumps and spins to look back at us. "OK, let's go."

Several doors slam, then I'm in the back seat with Sara, who smiles, leans over and gives me a shoulder nudge. I gaze at the passing houses. I know she wants a response. For the first time, I don't want to show Sara I love her. I'm not supposed to be here. I wish for a crash, killing one, and sending three to the hospital with minor injuries. I am too close. I don't want her to start getting suspicious, so I meet her eye. Her eyes blink wide. Her face is glowing like we are going to the mall to see Santa. Maybe she asked Lori about being gay, and then they started analysis on me. They're probably watching me. My empty stomach brings up bile, burning the back of my throat. I swallow it down.

"Happy Birthday, honey," saves me from talking to Sara. Mom leans over, and Lori on cue, leans and kisses her mom's cheek. The exchange makes me think of Mom. I'll have to plan another kiss. "How was the party?"

"Fine, Mom. This is Darby Saunders," Lori says as she turns around, as if she is making sure I am still there.

"So, this is Darby Saunders?" she says glancing up in the rear-view mirror and smiling confirmation.

Am I on display?

"Lori's mentioned you several times, so it's nice to finally meet you. I'd like to thank you for helping Lori with her math."

"It's not a problem," I say, wondering if Lori told her mom that I'm this wounded puppy, a math geek… someone she feels sorry for… so she keeps trying to include me. Is she showing off that she finally succeeded?

"We've heard you play several times, Darby. You're a very talented musician! Lori played the saxophone in middle school for two years; she still has it. Then she grew four inches and decided her future was putting balls over and into nets. Did she tell you she played?" I get another look from the rear-view mirror.

"No, she never mentioned it." I feel I need to change the topic. "I'm not sure how Sasha will behave at the bark park, because I've only known her for two days. I've never seen her with other dogs. She can be pretty friendly."

She pulls in and drives up to the door. "I'll keep a close eye. She'll be fine won't she, Pepper? I promise she'll be fine. I can tell she's a happy girl. Enjoy your brunch. We'll be back to pick you up in an hour or so."

32

"Let's get a booth," Lori says as she leads the way past the first four to the last one. Lori and Sara slide in one side. I am the loner.

The young waitress, holding a coffee pot, says, "Great game last night, Sara." The aroma reminds me of Mr. Buckley spilling his. "It's always great to beat Rothesay! You guys want menus? The special is two eggs any style, bacon, or sausage, toast, tea coffee."

I look at the waitress. I've seen her a hundred times walking the halls. Her name tag says Molly. I really need some water. I hope this doesn't take too long.

"We'll have menus," Lori says. "I'll have coffee please."

"Darby, would like a coffee?" Molly asks. The sound of my name makes me look up at her. I want to say that it's not fair. You're not supposed to know my name. Like you, a nameless person walking the halls, we're not supposed to know each other.

"Molly" – using her name makes us equal again, even though I'm cheating – "I'd really like a pitcher of water please."

"A little dry this morning?" she says with a smile.

Why is she smiling? "I guess so," I say, instead of 'I have this stomach backwash hanging on the back of my tongue and I can't risk another swallow till I get it rinsed.'

"Sara?"

"I'll have a coffee too please," Sara says, flipping up her cup, "and a glass to share some of Darby's water."

"There you go then. I'll be right back."

"Get whatever you want," Lori says.

There is a silence as we pretend to read, because everyone knows their favorite restaurant breakfast. I hear ice tinkle on glass. I look up.

"There you go, Darby." Molly pours. The first mouthful I swish around my cheeks, then under my tongue. With a gulp, I down the glass. I close my menu.

"Are you all ready?"

Eggs fried over-easy, bacon, toast. Eggs scrambled, bacon, pan fries, whole wheat. Eggs scrambled, whole wheat, extra bacon.

I gaze around to avoid eye contact. The place is a quarter full and a quarter dirty. Three quarters men with men, one quarter men with women. We're the only table of girls. It seems we're the only ones not talking. I look at the clock – 10:59. It's too late. I start thinking of anything that might have to be redone or changed, besides kissing Mom, leaving Sara happy, and leaving Lori on a positive note. I'm good. There'll be a chance tomorrow. I can't go back to school.

I fork my eggs around to make sure they're not runny. Sara and Lori are talking about Rachelle, who kind of ditched them at the party. It was so crowded that you had to elbow your way to the bathroom. When you got there, you couldn't get in, so they slunk around to the master bedroom looking for the ensuite. Joanna was in there with Barry. The kitchen floor was a soup of beer and snowmelt.

Silence. I look behind me, pretending I'm looking for Molly.

"Darb…" Lori waits. I have to turn back. "Last night Sara asked me about the day Rachelle upset me at lunch."

I look across at Sara. I feel a conspiracy. She keeps her eyes on Lori – I'm not supposed to know the result of their conversation. The promise that it would take place was all I needed. How do I say 'That's nice. You don't need to tell me because I already know; your secret isn't going anywhere with me. I did my part. Sara knows. You two are bonded now by a secret that will forge a forever friendship'?

"Anyway, it's true. It's the way I am, or who I've decided to be. The fact is, I don't know which. I don't know if my mom knows. I think she has her suspicions but I'm not sure. I think she'll still love me no matter. My Dad, well, he uses 'cocksucker' and 'that faggot' when he yells at other drivers. I can't risk him finding out. I'm not ready for the whole school thing either. I'm just happy that I'm spending my seventeenth birthday with you two… knowing." At the end, Lori's voice starts to shake.

Please don't cry. What do I say to stop it? Sara, say something. Sara keeps on eating, looking past me like she's riding shotgun for the conversation. The first tear rolls. I watch it fall off her cheek. "It'll work itself out. Your mom loves you. I can tell. She'll help you with your dad." Lori wipes her eyes with her napkin. "Old men see what they want and he'll never know unless someone tells him."

"I'm sorry for crying," she says. A sniff. "Last night at Sara's, she told me it was really you who noticed I needed help and that she was just doing the talking. You're right, Rachelle is a fucking bitch sometimes. Anyway, thanks, that's all I want to say. I'll never mention it again." Lori smiles through her tears. "There's not supposed to be any crying in baseball… or at birthday parties. These are the last tears about this," Lori says wiping her face, but the evidence is still there.

I look at Sara. She knew she wasn't supposed to let on that I knew. Sara's looking into her plate, and for the first time I feel like she betrayed me. Lori will cry when she finds out I'm gone and that wasn't supposed to happen.

33

Hiding in Plain Sight

We push through the glass doors out into the parking lot. The sky has become shades of grey. It'll probably snow soon.

How am I going to hide this afternoon? I'm not getting involved in a girls' movie party, spending my last day giving them all so much fuel for gossip. Their egos will make them think spending my last day with them was planned. Dad and Davey will be home soon. I don't want to have to listen to yadda, yadda, umbrella, yadda, yadda, yadda, dog, yadda, yadda, you, yadda, responsible, yadda, yadda, later. Maybe I could stay at Buckley's… read, play some music…

Lori looks at me, then to Sara, then to her mom wheeling into the parking lot.

"I have another idea. Let's go snowshoeing out to Cassidy's old farm. We can haul the toboggan and slide down chin-bumper hill," I say. Sara looks up with shock at me making a suggestion.

"I don't have snowshoes," Lori says, sighing.

"Not a problem. I have a pair you can use," I say.

"OK, I'll go," she says.

Lori's confirmation is all I need. Sara doesn't even answer.

"OK, let's roll!"

"When we getting back?"

"Four or five," I say. I get in the back seat and reach through the wire dog barrier; a pink tongue seeks out any remnants of breakfast.

"How was brunch, girls? We had a great time at the park, didn't we Sasha?"

"Fine," Lori answers. "Mom, we're going snowshoeing out to someplace Darby knows about. I'll have to go home and get clothes. Can you drive me back to Sara's?" Lori looks back at me.

"Sara's house."

"Sure, but don't forget your grandparents are coming over for cake at five."

"We'll be back in lots of time," Lori says.

Now all I have to do is leave Sasha at Sara's in case Dad is home.

34

Avoidance

The car pulls into Sara's driveway. "Do you want me to drive you home, Darby?"

"No thanks. I'll get out here." I don't want the car in the driveway in case Dad's back. "I'll be fine. Thanks for the drive and for taking Sasha to the park. It was nice meeting you."

"We'll be right back," Lori says out of the window. I pass the leash to Sara. "It will be faster if you just take her into your house. Dad'll have a fit if I take her home. Hey, remember to change the loads," I yell from the end of the driveway.

Mom's car sits in the driveway. I look for signs of Dad and Davey; it looks like the coast is clear. I pull the stepladder open. I climb up and shim the toboggan down between the rafters. I stab it in the snow around the side of the garage, out of sight. The snowshoes are hanging on the wall. I get mine, and Mom's for Lori and throw them with the toboggan.

I push through the door. The radio plays in the kitchen. I grab my winter clothes out of the closet and throw them down the stairs. "Mom!"

"I'm upstairs."

"I'm going snowshoeing with Sara, Lori, and Sasha. I'll be back at supper."

"You want some lunch before you go?" Mom asks, coming down the stairs.

"I ate at Sara's," I say, not wanting to explain the restaurant. "Sara's waiting. I love you."

"I love you too."

I run down the stairs, peel off my clothes, and pull on three layers. A door slams upstairs. I hurry, grabbing my backpack, jackknife and matches. I walk down the hallway. My snowpants swish, swish with my steps. I open the door to the cold junk-room. I hear, "We won, Mom!" I keep moving out through the door. Big cotton-ball snowflakes have started to drift to earth. I walk along the side of the house like a rat running along the wall. Cutting around the corner, I grab the toboggan under one arm, the snowshoes under the other. I peek around to the front of the house; I walk on the far side of the driveway so the sight-angle out the front window will be greater. Turning down the road, I imagine Dad asking, "Is Darby downstairs?"

At the Buckley's I unlock the door and take my boots off. I hurry up the stairs. The phone is flashing. I decide to press the button before I reach in the dog-treat box.

"Darby, this is Sally. Just calling to say hi. Hope everything is fine. We had a good morning; got everything done and now we're out shopping. I just saw the brightest cherry-red umbrella. It reminded me of you so I bought it. I hope you like it! Looking forward to seeing you tomorrow."

I feel it's odd Sally would be thinking of me. She never mentioned Sasha. I can't replace a black-and-white umbrella that matches a golf bag with a red one. I open the fridge, search the shelves back to front top to bottom looking for something. On the second shelf, I see it – a dozen hotdogs.

35

All Down Hill

I look out across the frozen bog we have to cross. There are layers of snow falling. Up close, a wall of straight-down falling snow, then a section of snow hanging in the air. Behind that, a layer of snow coming down on a left to right angle. All fading into a fog of snow so that the trees on the other side of the bog are just a grey background.

"It's really coming down," Lori says, sweeping off the snow that has piled up on Sasha's back. "It feels like we are on a true winter adventure."

"Nothing like ambiance to make the experience complete," Lori says as she drops her snowshoes and looks at me. I go over to her; she places her foot in the harness and her hand on my back as I secure it. "Got it?" I ask, looking up. She watches so intently it reminds me of a toddler trying to learn so they can act grown up and do it for themselves next time.

"I think so." She puts her right foot in and kneels down.

Sara has already started walking across the bog with Sasha. "You walk like this." I lift my knee high and show her my toes dipping down through the space in the harness. "Kind of like marching. Just go ahead and follow Sara's tracks," I say, snapping my last harness closed. Lori marches off, staring down as if making sure her feet are doing what her brain is asking of them. I grab the toboggan rope and follow. Turning back to the road I yell, "Sara! I think you can let her off the leash now." Sara's hand goes for Sasha's neck.

Loose, she shakes, shedding the snow in her fur. She runs back, stopping to inspect Lori and then to make sure it's me last in line. "You'll have lots of stories to tell when Sally comes back," I say, managing to get a back pat in before she gallops back out over the frozen bog. Lori starts to run to catch up to Sara, her snowshoes throwing snow up behind her like a rooster tail. Then she screams; a splash of white erupts. Sasha runs over to the excitement. Lori is on her back, with Sasha washing her face, when I arrive. "They're not really designed for running, you fool!" I reach my hand down.

"I just had to try. Thanks." Lori's face is soaking wet with snowmelt and some dog wash. I pull Lori to her feet.

"Thanks."

I hear snow landing on my shoulders. I tilt my face to the sky. Snowflakes liquify on my cheeks. I catch one on my tongue.

Four of us stand in silence in the middle of the Renforth Bog. "Which way?" Sara asks.

I point a mittened hand. "That way to the end where the beavers have it dammed. You've been there before. Then up through the woods trail."

"Hi ho hi ho," Lori says as she falls in behind Sara.

I watch my best friend followed by her next best friend. They both will need help and they can get it from each other.

"Where are the beavers?" Lori asks. "Over there," I say, pointing to the snow-covered dome on the edge of the pond. "They are snuggled up inside, beavers lying on top of beavers, staying warm."

"Sounds like a lesbian party," Lori says with a laugh. "Should I knock?"

"Maybe the Indians called the males dicks, but because the fur traders were men, they just went with the term beaver. So, there are really dick water-rodents and beaver water-rodents," Sara says, pulling off her hat. "I'm sweating."

"I like it," Lori says. "Steam is rolling off the top of your head. You better hope the beavers don't see you or they'll be calling you in. What do you think, Darby?"

"I think you're right so we better get off the pond before we three beavers are propositioned by the beavers," I say. It's the first time I've ever heard an openly gay person joke about sexuality. A thought comes to the surface of my mind.

Do mothers share their 'special love' with their daughters? Maybe, but if so, it too most likely goes to both graves. Nobody knows these things. A silent world, where the truth is more dangerous than the lie.

"Let's go."

"Uh, you bring any water, Darby?" Sara asks.

"I did, but there's a spring just a minute up the trail. I'll lead so you can rest a bit. Sasha c'mon." And into the cover of the woods we go. At the spring, Lori does a pushup pose over the trickling water. She lowers her lips to the water coming from the bowels of the earth.

"Shit that's cold! It makes my teeth ache," she says, coming up for air. She lowers herself for another fill. "I wonder what time it is anyway?" she asks as she stands. Sara tries to take her turn, but Sasha has decided to inspect Sara's apparent interest in the ground.

"Control the beast, Darby."

"Come on Sasha." I give her a tug.

Lori starts down the trail. "I'll lead, OK?"

The snow lies on the top side of all the naked hardwood branches; the evergreens have started to bow down with the weight of snow. The animal tracks have become smooth indentations in the new snow cover.

"It's a monochromatic world, everything is a shade of the grey sky. Even the green trees are not green," Lori says, turning her head back. "It's my favorite style to paint. I've never really seen it in except in moonlight. It's so surreal. Look I can see the hill."

"You're an artist?" I say.

"Sort of. I'm doing an independent study this semester," Lori says, stopping to face me. "Come on down to the art room at noon next week and I'll show you some of my work."

I always wanted to take an art class, but Dad picked advanced math. We walk out onto the abandoned pasture that slopes up from trees to gray horizon. We walk along the road that is cut into the side of the hill, and runs the entire length, about a hundred meters from the base of the hill.

"We'll climb here," I say as we reach the spot where there is a run-off for the toboggan. "We'll walk up the hill side-by-side and our snowshoes will make a trail for the toboggan, so let's try to stay in a straight line."

"How far is it?" Lori asks.

"It's a ways," I say.

"It stopped snowing. Wow, look, you can even see blue sky behind the clouds," Sara says. "You can see the top of the hill. It *is* a ways up there."

After one stop to open our jackets, and once for me to breathe deeply, we reach the top. Our trail is a scar on the virgin white cover. We push our snowshoes into the snow. I take my pack off and hang it on my shoes. I turn. Lori is holding Sara's hand. Her other is extended for mine.

"I want you to do something with me," she says.

I reach my hand out and she grasps it firmly around my palm.

"Come here with me." We walk a few steps out into the fresh snow. "Turn around, spread out, so our arms are spread. OK, now one two three, sit down." We plunk flat on our asses. "Now lay down and without letting go, make a snow angel."

My arms and legs swing. I can see the blue sky breaking through. I can't remember the last time I made an angel. Together we stand, and look down: our shadows loom over the indentations. Dog tracks show Sasha didn't get left out.

Lori, smiling ear to ear, takes out her disposable camera.

"Just a second." Sara pulls off my hat and then Lori's. She runs around the angels and puts our hats on the indented heads, signing our artwork.

"Now, can I?"

Sara and I stand, arms around each other's shoulders. I hold her as tight as I dare. I can feel her squeezing. Lori takes three pictures. "Great. Now let's conquer this hill!" Lori says as she pushes her camera into her pocket.

We load onto the toboggan. I am up front, then Lori, then Sara.

Lori looks around over my shoulder, says, "Holy fuck Darby! It looks pretty fucking steep. Are you sure? We're gonna kill ourselves!"

"Don't worry; we have the snow angels watching over us. Hang on."

"Let's bounce!" Sara says.

"If there isn't a little danger, there's no adventure," I say, laughing. "OK… push!" We all paddle our hands on the snow. Sasha starts barking. The snow under the toboggan squeaks as we inch forward, then gravity takes over. Sasha runs alongside. The toboggan picks up speed and we leave Sasha behind. The new powder sprays in my face. I have no idea if we are on the trail. Lori screams like we are on a roller coaster. I feel her grip on my waist. I hear Sara laughing. We must look like a white comet swizzing down the slope. I can feel the toboggan's bottom bending and flexing its way over the snow. I try to wipe my eyes but it's no use. I squint into an abyss of white. I start to panic that we're going to hit a tree if we don't stop soon. I grab the curve of the toboggan. Maybe it's time to tip it over before we start bouncing off alders. Then we are weightless. The road cut has launched us. I come to rest on my back, eyes closed.

Lori whoops, and Sasha starts to lick my face. I push her away to get to my feet. "Where's Sara?"

"Over here! I can't believe we just did that. I have snow down my neck, up my sleeves, in my ears. It was wild."

Three of us shake and brush snow off.

"Now what?" Lori asks.

"You and Sara trek it back up the hill. I'll head over to where the trail enters the pasture. There's blowdown there. I'll make a fire and we'll have hotdogs before we head back."

"You brought hotdogs? You're crazy!" Lori says.

"I'll see you in ten minutes. Come on, Sasha."

At the blowdown I strip some birch bark, snap branches off a dried pine that made its last stand against the Atlantic winds. I manage to get some good-sized splinters from where it split from the trunk. The birchbark curls from the heat of the match and black smoke rolls off. The pine crackles to life. I hear two voices coming as I snap off three alder branches to spear the hotdogs.

"My knife and the hotdogs are in my pack," I say. Sara passes me the backpack. I strip the branch, impale a dog and hand the branch to Lori.

"You're just like a Girl Guide, Darby. You know, this is wild. It's the first time I was ever on snowshoes, stood on a frozen beaver pond, drank from the earth, and told anyone who I am. It's a beautiful day! But I *have* roasted hotdogs on a stick before." Lori says as she watches her dog swell. She rolls it over.

"Darby likes the risk factor," Sara says, as she blows on her hotdog.

I look into the flames. Lori's secret is out in the open now, and she and Sara are sharing the happiness of acknowledging a beautiful thing. My secret is not like that. It can't be shared or fixed. There's only pain. I'm alone. I glance at the two of them biting dogs from a stick. Lori's eyes find mine. She holds them like she did in the cafeteria that day. Does she know what I'm thinking? I have been here too long. I have to leave tomorrow.

36

Finally

Lori's vehicle is waiting at Sara's as we drag our feet into the driveway. The lowering sun has turned our moist bodies into cold damp masses. Sara's mom comes out the front door, stands in the doorway.

"Looks like you had quite a day there, pumpkin," Lori's mom says. "You'll have to say goodbye because we have company waiting. We have to get going." Lori rubs Sasha's ears.

Her cheeks are rosy and wet hair clings to her forehead. I decide to let her go first. She takes a step towards me and gives me a one-arm hug. She whispers "thanks" in my ear.

I whisper, "You're welcome."

Lori steps back and hugs Sara.

The two of us stand watching them back out of the drive. The horn toots and we wave.

"You want to stay for supper, Darby?" Mrs. Campbell yells.

"No thanks; Mom and Dad are going out and I have to get home."

"So, what are you doing tonight?" asks Sara.

"Nothing, just dog-sitting and reading."

"Well, the first thing I'm doing is having a nap." Sara heads for her door. "I'll talk to you later."

I watch her for a few steps. "I love you."

"I love you too," she says without turning around.

I start to drag my stuff home. I can finally get on my way.

37

Outsmarted

"I gotta drop you off, then get home. Got it? Dad can vent a little bit at supper, but he's always a little gentler in a crowd. If I don't show up, Mom will call." Sasha changes from a walk to a trot. "No, you're not coming. If you did, I'd have to leave you out in the garage and that wouldn't be good enough for you or him, Mom, or Davey." I step over the snowplow's wake into the driveway.

I have to pull off my boots because my wet socks have air-locked them on. "OK now, let's see." I take off my coat, hat, mitts, and snowpants. "OK girl let's have some supper." I fill the bowl. Sasha eats. I fill her water dish. Sasha drinks. I turn on the TV and the lights. I have a pee, while Sasha guards the door. I find the squeaky toy on the living room floor. I toss it in the air and Sasha grabs it. I fluff the pillows on the couch and lay down. "I think it's nap time." I watch a car commercial. Sasha watches me. A Viagra commercial begins. I get up and walk downstairs. Sasha follows, squeak, squeak.

I open the kennel, say, "It's nap time." I quickly close it behind her. "Sorry about the manipulation, but often things aren't as they seem. I'll be back in a couple of hours, OK? You'll be fine. He's someone you don't need to know anyways."

Should I leave on the lights and TV? No, Sasha is not that dumb. I pull my boots on. My mitts are too wet to wear. I drape my snow pants over my arm.

"See ya girl."

38

Quality Time

√ Earrings
√ Hug
√ Supper plans
√ Saxophone
√ Clean out Locker
√ Library Books
√ Necklace
√ Mail letter
√ Skip History/write letter
√ Lunch with Sara/Lori
√ Ice cream
√ Mr. Frank
√ Supper
√ Talk to Sara about Lori
√ Clean room
  Breakfast with Mom
  ~~Leave~~
  Buckley's- note about dog Feed dog, take to Sara's
  Pack up stuff
  Leave

I put the toboggan and the snowshoes away without Dad hearing and coming out to the garage. I go through the upstairs door. If Dad is upstairs, I can judge the mood before I say I need to change.

"Hi Mom," I say, entering the kitchen. Mom's in her housecoat carving a roast chicken. The smell makes my mouth water.

She turns at the waist, leaving her hands over the counter. "Look at you all rosy-cheeked and soaking wet. Looks like you had a day."

"It was OK. Where's Dad?" I say, reaching for a raw carrot, needing to confirm that he's not downstairs.

"He's having a nap. I'm just waiting ten minutes before I get him up for supper. Davey is in his room watching TV. Who's Lori?"

"She's a volleyball girlfriend of Sara's. You two still going out?" I know the answer because of the housecoat.

"Yes, you know your father."

Why she doesn't say, *No, I'm tired. I worked this morning, I went sliding with Darby, I cooked supper. I want to stay home and sing with Darby.* Because she can't. I can't. Neither of us can. He got us both as puppies and we just obey the master.

"So, I left Sasha over at the Buckley's. I still plan on staying there tonight." I want to reconfirm with her so I can have a little backup at supper in case it does come up, but hoping it doesn't. Mom never lies but she's good at avoiding conflict, so she probably never told.

"Why don't you wait 'til after we leave and Davey gets settled a little. He was over at McGuire's this afternoon so he hasn't napped. He'll fall asleep watching the hockey game in bed."

"OK. I'll do that. He can call later if he needs me. I want to have a warm shower."

"Be quick; Dad will want you at dinner."

My door has moved. I look around – nothing has been returned to its place. My bed is still a mass of crumpled blankets. My eyes survey the closet. I check the dresser; the second down is pushed to the jam. I pull it open. I can't tell, it's all still folded black satin, black cotton, red, red, beige, beige white, white.

I'm the last one to the table. I serve myself and sit, forks colliding with knives scraping across ceramic. Mom places the fork of chicken in her mouth. Davy is maneuvering his carrots so they don't touch his potatoes. I reach for the salad.

"Darby, I told you no dogs. Don't ever bring it back here again! Where is it now."

"Darby has a dog?!"

"No, honey, she's just taking care of the neighbours' dog for the weekend," Mom says.

"When was he here? How come I didn't get a chance to see him? No fair!"

"Because Darby snuck it in her room last night after we were in bed," Dad says.

"She's home. I won't bring her back. I'm sorry," I say.

"Good. I don't want to see a single dog hair upstairs or down. You can take care of that tonight and I will be locking the downstairs door from now on," he says, staring at Mom.

I know he'll be downstairs tonight to check. I pray mom hasn't mentioned I'm staying at the Buckley's. "I'll take care of it right after supper." I try to keep eating and looking at him so I can be done when he is, and I don't hear *are you listening to me young lady?*

"I see my umbrella was out in the snowbank Friday morning. I got that when I was in South Carolina. Can you explain what in God's name made you think you could walk to Sara's in a gale? Why did you think the buses were running an hour late? Sometimes I wonder what in hell you're thinking and what your mother is thinking for letting you do it."

I'll tell what I was thinking. *I can't stand seeing you all happy the morning after you fuck me and having Mom kiss me and tell me she loves me with you at the breakfast table, because she does and I can't tell her that she has not protected me from you, because she would die. Her life and Davey's life have all been built on lies. Tonight, I am going to hide on you and tomorrow I am leaving and you won't get your last chance. I will be gone and the monster will die. Mom will find me and hold me and when she asks why it will be you seeing Mom every day knowing.* I spear two carrots off my plate.

"Sara and I went umbrella shopping this morning but they only had cherry-red ones," I say. "I'll replace it from the Pro Shop this spring."

"A red one, what in hell am I going to do with a red one?" he says getting up from the table.

I'm relieved that he got that out without bringing up babysitting. I look over at Davey. "How was the game today?"

"Great, we won and we play in the finals at noon against St. Stephen."

"Score any goals?"

"No. Yesterday I got the winner, top shelf, where mama keeps the cookies," he says, downing his water as he heads for the counter.

"Well good luck."

"No luck, all skill. Thanks anyway."

"What time are you going to church tomorrow, Mom?"

"Eleven, then I'm going out to breakfast with your aunt Mary. Would you like to come?"

"Yeah, sure."

I get up from the table.

"Davey, I want you to stay and help me with the dishes," Mom says.

"How come Darby doesn't have to? It's always me."

"Darby has to go down and clean her room."

I reset my room. Turning the knobs, I refocus my telescope on Alpha Orionis, done.

I sit looking at an Adams Number Eight Dry Fly clasped in the vice. I unscrew the vice jaws; the fly floats down onto my palm. I swing the magnifying glass over it. My fingers find the forceps lying on the desk. The harpoon tip of the hook looks fierce under the lens. The forceps squeeze down, smoothing out its prick point. Twirling the fly by its eye, I place my left hand under the lens. I decide on the tender inside skin at the bottom of my middle finger. I roll my finger to focus on the perfect profile. My skin indents, resists and accepts the tip. I push, slow and easy, watching the steel sink in, until I get what I need – a single drop of blood. As slowly as I entered the hook, I withdraw it. I suck the drop that's run into my palm. I grab a Kleenex.

I turn to the red numbers: 8:06.

Tomorrow will be the day. I have nothing left to do. When Dad doesn't find me tonight, he'll make some excuse to be alone with me tomorrow. It'll be easy to get out of going to church. Even if they both take vehicles, the ATVs will do fine. I can hang some plastic from the rafters to confine the exhaust. The sleeping pills might do the trick on their own. I hear sock feet on the stairs… Mom. I fold the list, tuck it in the desk drawer. I grab a hairbrush and bend over letting my hair fall over my head. My door opens. I toss my head up and my hair whips back over my head.

Mom stands in a red blouse and black hose. "Hi, honey, I was looking for something to wear. Dad suggested the skirt we bought that you wore to Mary's wedding. Do you mind?"

"Let me get it. Were you in here today? Because I can't find my gold bracelet."

"No, honey I wasn't. Maybe you left it at school."

It has to be Dad. What's he looking for? "Maybe." I reach in and bring the skirt out of the forbidden zone. "You want me to run the iron over it?"

"I'm sure it's fine if it fits. You know it looked so nice on you. Why don't you ever wear it to school?" she says as she steps into the skirt and shims it up over her hips. "The moment of truth."

"I think it fits," I say. "You could just wear your flat black leather belt, tuck in the blouse, or both."

Mom looks in the mirror, unzips and tucks. "How does it look; can you see any lines?" Turning sideways, she tries to get a look at her ass.

"No. Mom, you look like you just stepped out of *Vogue*. Not to worry about where those other bitches shop 'cause you're the only one sayin' 'Oh I got this from my daughter's closet.'"

"I guess there's something in that… I told Davey you'd be next door. He has the number. I looked in and he's already sleeping." She leans in. "OK, give me a kiss. Your father is on a schedule."

I reach for a hug, breathe her in and kiss her cheek. There was so much that we both should've said, so many questions we both should've asked. After a while, you just can't explain.

"Tomorrow, after lunch, we're going to find that old guitar. I'll see you tomorrow."

Sitting on the edge of my bed, I listen. I hear the gin bottle on the glass and Dad's tone rising and falling as Mom walks around, "she… better…you… late… lovely… Mary… damn dog."

"We're leaving, honey," Mom yells down the stairs.

I hesitate, thinking I didn't plan for last words. My boots walk down the hall. The door closes. "OK. See ya."

I retrieve my stash of pills, get the sax mouthpiece and put them in my purse, find my sleeping bag in the cold-room. I peek in Davey's room; he has the blankets pulled up to his chin; they rise and fall with his breath. I see his dreams of being a champion, Mom and Dad in the stands, proud of perfection. I close the door.

I set my sleeping bag on the workbench, straddle the ATV, turn the key; it putt-putt-putts to life. I turn it off. I check the other one. The staple gun hangs over the work-bench. I pull open the handle, slide the sleeve of staples out and back in. With two hands, I compress the handle and shoot a staple off the wall. In the rafters is the roll of plastic we used as a vapour barrier for the floor in my room. I visu-alize using two existing walls for two sides and plastic for the other two. If I use the section that has a ceiling, it'll fill up even quicker. It should only take half an hour to set up. I open the garage door to air out the smell of the exhaust. I remember my list is in my desk. I run back downstairs, pull the list from the drawer and stuff it in my back pocket. The room is perfect. Mom won't have to clean, wash, or look for anything. I pull the door shut and turn the knob so the latch catches.

39

The Cost of Business

"You have a nice nap? Sorry I'm late, there were some minor complications but it's all working out. Sally will be back tomorrow and you'll be back in the routine." I swing the door open. Sasha bolts out; she wriggles, jumps and pushes up against me. I give her a body rub. "It's only been a few hours, babes. Let's go upstairs and you can go out for a pee before we settle down for the night." Sasha runs up the stairs. I go two at a time behind her. I find her in the kitchen, looking at her dish. "Out first." I slide the door open; out she goes.

I go back into the living room and roll my sleeping bag out on the couch. I wonder what there is for snacks; I check the cupboards: chips, popcorn, granola; the freezer: pizza, eggrolls, butterscotch ripple, and Dilly Bars, bonus; the fridge, nothing much.

RUFF... RUFF...

"Let's go check the garage. We need some wood for the night." I pull on my coat. Sasha grabs her leash. "No walk, we're just going to the garage." I click the light. The Jag is on one side; boxes, a set of weights, mountain bikes, kayaks, BBQ, skis, and lawn furniture, are scattered in front of me. "Aren't we in luck tonight, girl." I pick my way around the stuff to the wood ranked against the back wall. Some split kindling is in front of the Jag. I count seven cedar sticks. I use my right hand to pick up wood and place it in the hook of my left arm. I pick up two pieces of White Birch; it's dry and dusty. I select four medium pieces, then I scan the rank for the largest pieces in the pile. I get two. "OK, this should keep us warm and comfy. We know where the pile is if we need more. Let's get in the house."

The flames rising from crumpled newspaper weave up through the crisscrossed cedar and reflect off Sasha's eyes. I pat her head. I balance the white birch on the pile of flaming cedar. I leave the door open a crack so I can smell the tarry black smoke of bark consumed by the flames. "Now the plan is to spend the night together. We're going to stay up, play a little sax, snack, watch a little something on Netflix, snack, finish the book, snack, go for a sunrise walk, then say goodbye. No more bad dreams for me! So, while we wait for the fire to warm us up, let's try the sax."

I eyeball the reed onto my mouthpiece and cinch it down. I grab the bell. It's cool under my fingers; I feel lines of scrolling in the bronze finish. Its weight makes me use two hands. I turn the bell – "Selmer Paris 54 Alto." I hook it up before I drop it. I slide on my mouthpiece. Filling my lungs, I push air. The G note flows from the bell. It's deep and rich, not as bright as mine. I noodle the G scale. My eyes close and *Baker Street* fills the room. Sasha barks and runs upstairs, where she continues to bark. I unhook the sax. I look up the stairs. Sasha has her paws on the door, barking at the window. "What's going on, girl? Someone in the yard?" I bet they came home early. I place the sax back in the stand. "OK, I'm coming, just a second. They'll be in in a second." I get to the top of the stairs, grab Sasha's collar, and pull her down from the door.

Sara waves at me through the window.

"What are you doing?" I say as I open the door.

"Well, I had a nap, and when I woke up it was dark. Mom was already in bed. I called your house; no answer, so I decided to walk over and then when I got this far, I saw the light and the smoke from the chimney." Sara bends down to rub Sasha's ears. "Anyway, I figure we can watch some TV or just hang out for a couple of hours."

"Sure, why not." I back away from the door. "Sasha, give her some room so she can get her shoes off." I grab her collar and lead her into the living room. The black logs are a mass of flames, the fan has come on; air blows out the vents. I open the door and place another log on top, causing sparks to fly out the door. I quickly close it. I fold up my sleeping bag and throw it on the chair. This won't be so bad. Sara's company will help pass the time. She'll probably leave around midnight, one at the latest. She won't spend the night.

Sara walks into the room, stands in front of the fire with her hands stretched out. She turns her backside to the flames and puts her hands behind her. "That feels good," she says. "Everything OK? I could hear the sad sax sounds coming from the basement," she says.

"The sax is always a sad sound, that's why it's called da blues!" I say, sitting down on the couch. Sasha's lying on her dog bed, her head up. I think she's anticipating another guest or some sort of move by Sara. Sara walks over. I know she's going to sit beside me because she's always been one for snuggles. Not so much now, but when we were younger, she'd hold my hand when we walked around the playground. She had a blanket, her "baba." She'd cover us up with it as we watched Harry Potter. She'd stroke my earlobe between her thumb and finger. I can remember her doing it and how sensual it was, but I can't remember when she stopped. I spent March Break at her house once. She moved into the spare room with me. She fell asleep on her side of the bed, but often when I woke up, her arm was over me. On the school bus, she'd move the books or book bag from between us. Sara sits. The couch sags, bringing our shoulders and hips together. She reaches for the remote and clicks on the

TV – hockey, commercial, *Saturday Night Live*, *Kids in the Hall*, Peter, Paul and Mary. We listen.

"I'm gonna do a tour," she says. "You wanna come?"

Tour is really a code word for 'I'm gonna do a superficial snoop'. Is there any porn on the bedroom nightstand or in the DVD collection? What kind of liquor's in the cupboards? Are the beds made? What hangs in the closets? Make-up check, pictures on the walls, snacks. "I'm fine; already did the cupboards. There are Dilly Bars in the freezer; you can bring us back one. Don't move any stuff around, and don't touch the instruments." Sasha jumps to her feet as Sara stands. "You going too?" Sasha looks at Sara going up the stairs. She lies back down and sighs.

Holy shit! I remember the note on the kitchen table. I listen. Shit, shit, shit! The kitchen lights flick on. I walk up the stairs. Sara's reading the reminders, messages, and stuff on the island. I glance at the note. I look at Sara while concentrating on not looking back at it. "Why don't you get us a Dilly Bar?" Sara pulls the freezer door open, hiding her face. I move to block her view of the table.

"This is a bonus." Sara passes me a bar. I peel the wrapper and pass it to her.

"The garbage is under the sink," I say. Sara turns her back. I turn mine and grab the note. I cough, shove it in the envelope and stuff it down my shirt. Instead of falling to my waist, it lies against my breasts. Shit! I pull at my shirt, lean forward and shimmy, trying to get it over them.

"What are you doing?"

"Brain freeze," I say.

"Your brains are in your bra?"

"Some ice cream fell down there and there's a lot of flesh to freeze," I say. I feel the envelope scratching my tummy. Is it visible through my shirt? I sit at the table.

"I'm going upstairs, coming?"

"No, been there."

When Sara heads up, I return to the fire. I pull the envelope out, open the door. I watch through the door making sure it burns; the fifty reveals itself for only a second before it too is gone.

"Not too much exciting," she says, coming back down the stairs. "They drink beer. Someone likes gin; there's a gallon of it over the sink. She's a smoker. She has nice clothes and a dozen pairs of boots. Lots of unpacked boxes; the juicy stuff's probably in there. No TV in the bedroom, which is a good thing. I never knew there was a hot tub in the backyard. What's downstairs?"

"Not much – a bunch of musical instruments, Sasha's kennel." I sit back on the couch. Sara flops beside me and picks up the remote. Peter, Paul and Mary, commercial, hockey, *Saturday Night Live*, *Kids in the Hall*. The silence grows. She wants me to bring up Lori. I decide to leave it alone.

40

"Hey Darby?"

"Yeah?"

"Let's get some drinks, snacks, and soak in the hot tub. I've never been in one in the winter."

"I don't have a bathing suit. I'd have to go back home."

"Me neither. Let's just wear our bras and panties. What's the difference? You can shove yours in the dryer if you don't want to go home au naturel. Let's do it! They have lots of towels."

I have my nude bra on, and white cotton panties. I'll get them soaked. I wonder how cold it will be. I've never even been in a hot tub before, inside or out. I shrug. "Sure. Why not."

Sara fills a bowl with chips. I cut some cheese and find some onion dippers. We decide on pop instead of hot chocolate, glasses and ice instead of cans. We uncover the tub, set out the food. I find two bath towels in the closet. We strip in the spare bedroom. Sara giggles like we are stealing the cookies my mom used to leave cooling on the counter. I shut off the outside light before I slide the door open. Sasha leads; the winter air cools my shoulders, the wind gusts. Every nerve in every crack, crease and pore of my body comes to life. I shift from one foot to the other as I hang my towel on the bar. I step down into the tub. Steam rolls up from the cauldron. Sara grabs my hand. I ease my way in; water covers my gooseflesh legs. My body slips down. The chlorine fills my nose. A sense of peace and relief washes over me as the heat takes the bite of winter away. I slouch lower so the water reaches my chin.

"This is the life. It feels like I want to have a nap," Sara says. Her feet float to the surface as she goes under the water; the jets push her over to my side. Her head bobs back up like a seal. She's wearing my chain.

"It's not a swimming pool," I say with a laugh.

Sara slips under again. I can see her moving back to her side. She comes up holding her bra and panties. "It might not be big enough for swimming, but I'm getting the whole experience." Flop, her soaked bra hits the deck.

I lift my feet; my head goes under; the jets push me across the tub. I reach behind my back and undo my bra. I come up on Sara's side. I reach under the foam and bend my legs out of my panties. I pass them to Sara.

"Isn't that better? It was kinda like having a sundae with no chocolate sauce," she says.

I let the jets take me back to the other side. I lay my head back on the rest, move my bum so the jet hits the center of my back, stick my toes in another and let my fingers play in yet another. The black sky is sprinkled with blue salt. My eyes widen, my stare becomes unfocused, my chest rises, falls, rises, falls. Sara's foot presses up against mine, bringing me back.

"Darby."

"Hmm?" I keep my eyes on the sky.

"I'm sorry for telling Lori it was you who told me. I knew you didn't want her to know. It was your fault in a way, because last night in my room you told me I was the leader, so lead. I get credit for things all the time that I really got help with." Sara's voice rises into a radio voice. "*High scorer for the Crusaders, Sara Campbell*, but they don't say two of Sara's friends, Lori and Joanna, passed her the ball thirty times or took on their best player, or set five picks causing them to bruise their asses. It's just Sara, Sara, Sara. This time I gave the credit where credit was due." Silence. I feel the pressure on my sole.

"It's OK, I still love you," I say.

"I still love you too."

I reach for my glass. The cold sensation runs out along my ribs as I swallow. I grab some chips. They crunch in my mouth and crumbs float in the tub. "I think chips might not have been a good idea," I say with a chuckle, causing a few more crumbs. I lay my head back again; I close my eyes. Car tires crackle and crunch on the street. The water rises to my ears, Sara's shoulder bounces off mine, then they settle against each other.

"Darby."

"Hmm."

"Have you ever worried about something 'til it made you sick?"

I don't think she really wants an answer. She has something she wants to tell me. "Yeah, I guess so, but I can't really remember," I say.

"I have, since I was in Grade Seven – Mrs. Jamieson's Family Living class. You remember when you were in Grade One, and I was in Grade Two?"

"Yeah sure," I say. Is this Sara coming out? I turn to face her. Sara looks straight ahead.

"Go ahead, Sara, I'm listening." I turn my head back to the stars. "Tell me. You saw how happy Lori was today knowing her worries were shared."

"Funny you should say that, because I was thinking the same. So I want to tell you something. As a matter of fact, I came here tonight to do it. When I was in Grade Two, Mom and Dad got divorced. Remember?"

"Sure, I remember."

"On the bus that day, you told me that your parents were never going to get divorced because you explained a special love you shared with your dad. I didn't have that love, so I tried to explain it to my dad so he wouldn't leave. He got mad, and told me I didn't understand, and you didn't know what you were talking about. For years, all I could think about was you had a dad and I didn't. Maybe because I didn't know how to love him special like you did. The squirting love… washing up in the creek; a special bond. It all sounded so great. When Mrs. Jamieson said, 'During ejaculation, semen squirts from a man's erect penis; it's a milky fluid,' all I could hear was you singing 'squirt, squirt, slime, slime' as we sat on the school bus that cold November day. So, I lay in bed wondering… is Darby being abused by her dad? I've watched you for signs of it. I wanted to ask you so many times. I figured your mom would know. I've lain in bed staring at the ceiling saying it can't be so. Darby would tell me. Darby…"

My eyes stay open. I was hearing, but it was like I wasn't listening. Why didn't I stop her? Instead, I'm in the truck pulling up and down on a penis saying, "Hurry, Dad. I want to go fishing"; feeling heat from my sleeping bag as it burned in the fire. I watch Mr. Peterson pulling his dick at Black Bear Pool, saying the old man didn't mind sharing. I hear Mom say "I love you" when I came back from fishing.

"Darby, is it true?"

I feel like a dish rag in warm water. I turn my head; my eyes focus on the turbulence in the tub. My gaze traces up Sara's arm and lingers on the chain floating at her throat. My chest rises and falls. I'm drifting. The irises in Sara's blue eyes have little lines of black running through them like they are cracked crystal. A dog barks. He must want to come in out of the cold. There's nowhere to hide, or for my soul to travel, no lie for 'love, stick, rub, slime, wash up, don't tell Mom.' Sara's eyes close; they open again.

"Yes."

One single syllable; her eyes dart. The syllable runs through the synapses of her auditory cortex, drifting into her amygdala, bouncing through her frontal lobes and her empathic processes. Her mouth droops, her eyes swell wide and fill; tears leak from the black cracks in her irises.

"Oh Darby."

My face stays like stone. Sara's head shakes in tiny no, no, no's. Her chin quivers into dimples. Her shoulders sag. She sinks lower. She stares at nothing. "I'm so sorry." Nothing but tears.

I reach my arm around my best friend and I pull her tight. Sara rolls into my chest, crying. I feel her naked body sobbing at the realization of the worst. I squeeze her harder. "It's OK, Sara, it's all over, it's all over; it's never gonna happen again." How many lies have I told her?

"I knew, Darby. I knew when I was twelve. I didn't say a word, I just kept it to myself. I could've helped."

"No. It wouldn't have changed anything. I had to make the change. Sit up. I'll tell you a secret." I straighten Sara up. I grab her two hands in mine.

"You're right," I tell her. "I've lived a lie for a long time. But it's all over. Thursday it ended. I'm going to tell you a secret you can never repeat. Friday, I gave my sax back, cleaned out my locker, bought ice cream for the gang, said goodbye to Mr. Frank, gave you my necklace, made pizza with my mom and hugged her tight, told you about Lori because she needs a best friend and you'll need one while I'm gone. Today I was supposed to leave; the Buckleys interfered, so this morning I was bringing Sasha over to your house so you could dog sit and I could get going."

"Where are you going?" Sara is shaking, her eyes are frantic and won't focus.

"Shhh. Then Lori was there and I couldn't explain it, then Lori's birthday, and I missed my time to leave. So, I'm leaving tomorrow when Mom's in church and Dad and Davey are in St. Stephen. I can't tell you where I'm going or how, because then you'll be pressured to tell, and that monster will hunt me down. It's a safe place, an underground organization. That's all I can tell you."

"Darby, you're scaring me." Tears reemerge. "Why don't you just tell your mom?"

"Mom can't stand up to him. I've tried, but I can't. Davey needs a dad. I've planned my escape for a year. I'm sure about this."

"This sounds crazy, this is fucking crazy Darby! Just stop for a second. Am I ever going to see you again? There is no way you can just go out the door and never come back." Sara stands, naked in the winter wind. She's as white as a ghost and shaking. "Please don't. There's gotta be a better way."

"You're gonna see me again, it'll just be a while. I promise." I reach to pull her down into the warmth. "Sara you're the only friend I've ever had. Promise me you won't tell."

"What do I say when people ask where you are? I'm not sure I can do this, or even want to. I don't know; more lies on more lies. How do I know you're safe and not just in more shit?" Sara covers her face with her hands. She looks up at me. "Promise. You call me when it's safe."

"Say, she didn't tell me where. She said goodbye last night like everything was normal…" I try to stay in the lie, and realize I am going to have to calm her down. I reach for a towel wishing this wasn't happening. "I'll contact you somehow, give me a week. Now, let's get out of this tub and talk inside."

I throw one of the big logs into the coals, and pull the draft open. Sara will cope; she knows the worst. I don't think she'll tell. She too has a guilty conscience. I should've just left this morning and kenneled up that damn dog. I look at the dog bed Sasha is stretched out on, on her side. My body feels tired but I don't feel any relief that Sara knows. Nothing changes except now Sara knows.

"They'll be dry in twenty minutes," Sara says, coming up the stairs. "Let's eat one of those pizzas."

I tell Sara I expect her to become a doctor and not to be slacking off just because I'm gone. She says by then we'll be best friends again. I say yes, we will. She tells me that she always thought I was the luckiest person in the world to have a mom and a dad, and all the money we seemed to have. She asks me how I was able to deal with it for so long. I tell her we are not allowed to talk about it on our last night. She tells me about punching Vanessa the day she came back from the divorce. I tell her about trying to skip Grade Eight so I could be with her in Grade Nine. I tell her about hiding in the band room at noon, pretending to practice. She says I could stay with her. I say it wouldn't work. She tells me about not going to her dad's for Christmas because it's payback. I tell how I used to wish her mom would ask me to stay for supper so I didn't have to go home. She tells me her mom thinks that she is the best clothes folder in the world. I tell her I don't think her mom is that stupid. She asks, what about my mom? I say it's the hardest thing about leaving. She tells me if I wasn't her friend, she wouldn't have talked about anything except sports and boys. I tell her I loved it when she used to rub my earlobe. She tells me about crying when I bought my first bra, and again when I had my first period, before she did. She asks if I'm sure about leaving. I say I am. I've been planning for a year and I have help. She asks who. I say I can't tell. I tell her I love her and I have a big day tomorrow. She'd better go. She says she doesn't want to, and starts crying. I tell her I'm sad but I'm not crying because it is what I know I have to do.

Sara wants to do the dishes, but I insist on doing them.

"Can I call you tomorrow?"

"Please don't," I say. "We're going to say goodbye face-to-face." I pass her her coat. Tears are coming again, for us both. I hug her. She squeezes me tight, and tighter; she won't let go. I loosen my grip, and step back.

"I want to give this back to you…" Sara reaches her hand around the nape of her neck.

"No. I really, really want you to have it. That was part of my plan, so giving it back will be bad luck."

She sticks her finger in her mouth, then twists off a ring her dad gave her when she was sixteen. It's a ruby set in gold. "I want you to take this with you."

"You sure?"

"Yes, I want you to have it." She takes my hand and places the ring in it.

I can only nod and say, "I'll keep it until I see you again." I look down to put it on my finger. I feel a hand slip under my hair and a finger and thumb rub my earlobe. I keep my head down, pretending I'm pushing the ring on. I swallow a memory. I look up, "It's time to go." I open the door.

Sara wipes her face, turns, and leaves. I close the door behind her, watch her go down the driveway and disappear as she walks through the streetlight's orange glow.

41

DOWN off the Roof

All the windows are dark on the backside of my house. I pull the drapes. The microwave says 12:53. "They're probably not home yet, girl." I look down. Sasha's eyes lock on mine, then dart to the dish in my hand. I pass her a pizza crust. I shut the kitchen lights off and head down to the living room. I click on my reading light, and stoke the fire. I return to the kitchen, turn on the light over the stove and start the dishes. Sasha sprawls on the kitchen floor.

"I'm exhausted, girl. I want to be in my sleeping bag. Do you think she'll understand that there's no way I could've told her the truth?" She whines and heaves a sigh. "I think she will; not at first maybe, but she will. We all get over things. She'll be busy being a student, a doctor, a wife and a mother." I open the dishwasher and rearrange the dishes so the plates are with the plates and all face the same way. "Let's go read." Sasha scrambles up and passes me on her way down the stairs.

I unroll my sleeping bag on the couch, pull on my grey sweats, lay in the fold and zip up. I lean my head back on the arm. Sasha finds her bed and looks up at me. I unzip, push the coffee table over, and put my sleeping bag on the floor. "OK, get up, girl." I pull on the dog bed. "Up babes." Sasha stands and her tail starts to wag as if in slow motion. I pull the dog bed over beside my sleeping bag. "There." I climb back in. I use two couch pillows to support my head and shoulders. The fire dances in the window, my right hand finds Sasha's silky ear, my left holds a book. "Now let's escape for a while." Sasha heaves a sigh. I start to turn pages.

My book hits my legs, my head jerks up. The fire has burned down. Should I get up? I feel Sasha's warmth all along my legs. I can't let myself fall asleep. Sasha lifts her head; she turns towards the door. She rolls over to her belly then gets to her feet. She's focused on the door. "What is it, girl?" Her body blocks my view. As I bend to look under her, barking erupts and she gallops to the door. Her barks are loud and become quicker and quicker. I hear her nails up on the door. "It's OK, Sasha. I'm coming. It's probably just Sara coming back." I kick my way out of the bag. "You're going to wake the whole neighbourhood!" I feel along the wall for the light switch. I squint to filter the light. The doorknob rattles. Sasha digs for more volume. "Calm down, calm down."

I look out. Dad's face is pressed up against the window. He rattles the knob. My heart is pounding; I reach out to the wall for support. Oh my God, oh my God, why isn't it Sara?

"Darby, control that damn dog! Let me in," he yells through the window.

I reach for the collar. "Sasha stop." She pulls away and jumps back onto the door. I get a better hold. "Sasha stop! I can't make her stop," I yell back. Please go.

"Open the damn door."

"OK, OK, just give me a second. Sasha stop, easy girl. It's OK, it's OK." I pat her back, get her down off the door. I reach for the knob. Dad takes a step back and staggers another step backwards before he rights his balance.

I breathe two heavy breaths and turn the knob. I can feel cold air coming off his body. Sasha barks. I feel safe holding her and don't want her to stop. "It's OK." Dad walks past us. I look down the stairs but I know the kennel will be a no. "Now we are going in there, and you be good." I walk into the living room holding Sasha's collar. Dad's sitting on the couch.

"Come here and sit with me, Darby." He pats the couch beside him.

I walk over. Sasha stops and stands on her bed. I step over my sleeping bag, pick up the pillows, put them between us and sit on my own cushion.

"This looks cozy. You camping out just like we used to do? Remember?"

"I remember." I think about the gin in the cupboard, but he isn't drunk enough that I can make him pass out. "How was the party?"

"It was alright. You know your mother; she talks and flirts like a twenty-dollar whore but looks like a hundred-dollar lay." I look over, having never heard him speak about Mom like this. "Then!" Dad's voice raises, "she got smart in the car." Sasha raises up onto her belly.

"Listen, Dad, the Buckleys are supposed to come home sometime tonight. I was just waiting up for them."

"Little girl, you and your fucking mother may think you're smart but you're not as smart as the old man. She already told me they're not coming back 'til tomorrow and another thing, you've been stealing something from my bedroom. I need those for your mother. She's dead to the world with those."

I look at my purse. "I don't know what you mean." I tell myself not to look again. Just let him ramble, don't fight.

"Yes, you do. I've been through every part of your room looking for those pills! But it doesn't matter, because tonight she's over there and we're here camping out. Just like old times." His hand reaches over and rubs down my cheek and then my breast.

Sasha's voice fills the room with two booming barks. "You shut up!" Sasha stands and continues barking; her front feet marching. "You shut up!"

Barking!

A kiss

Barking!

Get! Away! A pillow flies.

Barking!

I twist around his arm, get onto my knees. I rub my hands along her neck, "Please stop, shh – he'll leave." Sasha barks louder.

"Shut her up, Darby!"

Barking! "Dad, I can't." I start crying, wishing I could. "Please leave! We can do this tomorrow."

"Leave? I'm not leaving because of a dog."

Barking! I put my hands over my ears.

Dad gets up and Sasha backs away. Barking! Barking! Dad takes a swing at Sasha's snout. He misses, falling a step forward like a staggering fighter. Sasha keeps adjusting the distance and barking. Dad keeps swinging.

"Stop! Dad, stop! Let me get her. Please, Dad, don't hurt her. Dad!"

Sasha, still barking, backs herself into the corner between the chair and the wall.

Dad reaches out and grabs her by the scruff of the neck. I hear myself crying. He pulls the hide up, stretching it. Sasha's feet almost come off the ground. "Please Dad. I'll be good." This is no longer between me and Dad. With one mighty push, Sasha's head hits the floor.

I see her face between Dad's legs, saying, 'I have been a bad, bad dog.' I try to send her a message, 'No, no, I love you. You're a good girl; he's a bad person!'

"I'll teach you who the fucking boss is." He rubs Sasha's head into the rug. Dad drags her towards the stairs.

Sasha resists for a second, then goes like a convict being dragged off to isolation.

I want to get up. I want to free her. I want to tell her she is a good dog. I cry. I hear the door slide open. "Out you fucking bitch."

I wipe my face. I can't face him with tears. Dad staggers back down the stairs. "I would've stopped her," I say. He sinks into the couch. "Dad, I can't! Please, please, I want to but I can't tonight, not here. I promise we can go for a drive tomorrow after the hockey game. We can say we're going out for supper. It will be special."

He grabs me and pulls my shirt up. His pupils dilate. I watch his fingers spread wide. I hear Sasha's nails on the glass, BARK. My back hits the cold leather. BARK. My sweats go down. I look for some place for my soul to escape. I try the windows; the drapes keep me in. BARK. I search the ceiling for a pattern to focus on. None. BARK. I turn my head a little. A red ember still glows in a black space. I see it and I look into it, BARK. I'm with it and I can feel my soul go up the chimney. I'm above the house, surrounded by stars. BARK. I am teetering on the peak of the roof. I feel cold air. I hug Sasha to me.

OH, MY GOD! DARBY, DARBY. Mom is holding me so I don't fall.

"I'm safe here, Mom."

I feel her arms around me. "I'm here with you, Darby."

42

No Tomorrow

Blue lights whirl around the walls as though an alien space-ship has landed in the yard. This is another tipping point, like the day I lied to Mom about burning my sleeping bag. Like pushing that toboggan over the edge – once gravity catches it, you can't stop.

Who called the police? I guess there's only so much barking, screaming, yelling, and a neighbourhood mother walking into the new neighbour's house at two a.m. that a cul-de-sac can take before someone has to stop minding their own business.

A huge policeman with a bushy mustache stands in the living room with snow on his boots. I am going to have to clean it up before Sally gets home. A woman appears out of nowhere and wraps a blanket around my shoulders. "My name is Detective Rose; I'm a police officer. I'm here to help you."

"Where's my mother? Is she gone? Where's Sasha?"

"Your mom is right here with us, Darby. Everything is over; you are safe now," she says as she shifts so I can see Mom. "Is Sasha your dog?"

"No, she's the Buckleys dog." Mom sits slumped in the armchair wrapped in the same kind of blanket that is around me. She stares at me but her eyes don't acknowledge me. Detective Rose speaks into her microphone and garble comes back.

"Darby, is this your house?"

"No, I live over there." I point.

"Darby, was anyone else in the house earlier this evening?"

I wasn't really sure why they were asking. "Sara, and my dad." I say, hoping that they will leave so I can clean myself up. Detective Rose speaks into her microphone. More garble, then the house is flooded again with lights.

"Who is Sara?"

"My best friend."

"Her last name?"

"Campbell."

More police, and ambulance guys in white shirts.

"Darby, we are going to take you to the hospital."

"I'm fine. I don't think I need to go. I'm supposed to take care of the house and the dog 'til tomorrow." If they would all just leave, Mom and I could have a talk. I still have plans for tomorrow. A stretcher comes in. I start to cry. I can hear Mom weeping, and I realize tomorrow is not going to happen. "I'm OK, Mom." She sobs. I get up off the couch and walk around the stretcher, being careful not to trip. A hand steadies me.

"Excuse me," I say as I squeeze between a policeman and Detective Rose. I brush against the shoulder of a man in a suit. "I never leave my mom without kissing her goodbye." Her limp arms go around me.

"I am so sorry, Darby, I am so sorry. My baby, I'm so sorry."

"I know, Mom. I know. I'm alright. It's OK."

Outside, the ambulances, fire truck, police cars, and cars that didn't look like police cars, have whirling blue lights. Firemen carry the stretcher; no one looks down at my face. I am spun around and see faces strobing in blue. Their lips are moving, but I can't hear anything. Just before I close my eyes, I see Mrs. Campbell, her arm around Sara. I try to sit up and tell her I'm OK, but I'm tied down.

43

Exposed

The ambulance doors open; cold caresses my cheeks. Bumpy bump. Fluorescent light pierces my eyes.

"Darby, remember me, Detective Rose, from the house? I nod. This is Annabella. She's a social worker here, and we are going to help you through this. Your Mom is alright and she too is receiving some attention. Your aunt Mary is on her way. Mrs. Campbell is taking the dog, and Davey is being looked after."

I nod; start crying. Someone holds my hand.

The whole hospital experience… it felt like watching TV; I was seeing but not really attached. Everyone was calm and business-like. They acted like I understood what was happening. They took my clothes and put them in bags. I said "yes" when they explained what they had to do. I said, "OK, I understand." When the doctor did the internal examination, I closed my eyes and cried. I wanted my mother. Annabella held my hand. She told me it would be over soon. I could feel them brushing my pubic hair. "If you just stop, I'll tell you what happened," I said. "Please!"

"It's not that simple, Darby," Detective Rose said. "They're almost done. You can have a nice hot shower in a few minutes." I realize I'm not going home; tomorrow is not going to happen the way I planned.

I stand in the shower for an hour. No one checks. My head clears; silent tears roll off my cheeks. My thoughts start to race…the lie I told Sara, my purse is still back at the house, the list is inside it, my pills will be found, where had Dad gone to? He wasn't in the room when the policemen were talking. What's he going to do? What did they mean, Davey is being taken care of. How much shit Mom's going to have to take about this happening? She's going to have to tell Davey something. Sara will not lie. Is Sally going to find out? If I hadn't lied about that sleeping bag, this wouldn't have had to happen. How is Mom ever going to trust me again? How am I going to leave now that they know I want to?

I am pushed through silent halls and ride a confined elevator, in a wheelchair, wearing a hospital gown. Detective Rose and Annabella walk alongside. Silence.

"This is where we say goodbye and goodnight," the nurse says.

"Try to get some rest Darby. We'll be in to see you tomorrow," Annabella says. Rose is silent, smiling sadly.

"Thanks."

The room is dark. The sheets rustle in the next bed.

The nurse pulls the curtain over. "Here you go Darby, this will help you sleep."

44

A Dawning

When I wake up, the room is bright. A girl with cotton candy hair sits in the bed next to me. The remnants of two breakfasts sit on the table between us.

"I hope you don't mind, but I ate your waffles two hours ago, while they were hot. They'll bring you another," she says. "I'm Cathy."

"Darby. It doesn't matter. Mom will be here to get me soon."

"I have news for ya. You're not leaving here anytime soon. You just got here. The ward is locked."

"Locked?"

"You don't know where you are? You're in the Psych ward, girl – for cutters, non-eaters, eating-too-much-ers, overdose-ers, but mostly for fucked-up suicides. I looked you over while you were sleeping. You look pretty well maintained, so you're a probably a suicide gone bad."

"Yeah, pretty much."

Mrs. Campbell pushes through the door.

"Good morning, Darby dear. Hope you got at least some sleep. Here are a few things from home. There is something in the bag from Sara." She puts a suitcase on the chair. "Your mom will be in soon." She walks to the window. The room is flooded with sunlight.

"Where's Dad?"

"That's a family matter. Maybe talk to Annabella about that; she'll probably be in to see you a little later. Everyone is safe and wishing you the best. After you look through the bag, if there's anything else you want from home, tell the nurse. I don't work on this floor. Annabella is the person to tell." She turns and leaves like she is late for an appointment.

"You know her?" Cathy asks me, as she pulls a T-shirt over her head.

"Yeah, she's my best friend's mom."

"No shit. We might be able to get double dessert then! You're going to have orientation to the ward this morning and meet a bunch of people. I'm going to group. I'll be back at lunch." She presses a buzzer next to the door.

I dig through the bag until I find it and crack open the card. Two handwritten words 'Friends Forever' and our symbol of it. I put it around my neck. I look at the clock. 10:30. I am supposed to be gone. I walk into the bathroom and stare into the mirror. I am in the death zone, no future, no plan, the list is finished. I go back and sit on the bed. I fondle the chain. What do I do now? Where do I go? I flop back on the bed and close my eyes.

Annabella and I walk to meet Detective Rose and Aunt Mary. She'd said it was for a statement. I figure Mom asked Aunt Mary to come because she couldn't bear to herself, to feel the guilt. I am glad she's not here.

"I am going to record our meeting," Detective Rose says. "I am going to say a few things, then ask you a few procedure things." My eyes dart around; no one is looking at me. I hear dates, time, location. I re-swallow breakfast. "From the beginning, Darby, in your own words, can you tell us what happened please?"

I look over Aunt Mary's head, out the window. A cloud drifts, revealing the sun. I drift with it, to a dirt road and a truck. I land in the Buckley's living room. Not till I am finished do I look down. Aunt Mary's face is pale, glistening with tears. Annabella swallows, forces a smile and places a warm moist hand on mine. Detective Rose looks up from her notepad, pages deep. I heard her take a deep breath. She shuts off the equipment.

I don't need a hug or a kiss or a condolence. I want to go back to my room, climb back in bed, pull up the blankets and roll away from their faces.

45

Promise

I decide to never see him again. I'm going to be my mother's daughter now and I want Mom to know that it was her I loved; that he was never going to have the chance to separate us again. I was something he wanted. He was not seeing me again because I knew he would always be seeking some way to bump up against me, kiss me, smell me, rub his hands along my body. If he gets jail time, it would end eventually. He would play the game to get free. No; no weekends, no holidays, no parent-teacher, no supervised visits, no, no, no, never. I am supposed to be gone, so he was never going to see me again anyway.

I won't attend court. My statement was all they said I needed to do.

I need to start another list.

46

Group

I taped a photo of the three snow angels Sara sent me in the notebook I took to group. It helps me focus on my list, and I stare into it while I tell my stories. The truth: the social workers, psychologist, and group sessions won't change the fact that I kept secrets from the people I loved the most, and now Mom has only Davey to trust. I have no secrets left in my life. For all of us in group, it is not the drug use, the prostitution, and the other shit that we struggle with really. It's all ugly, in the past and it's the truth. Worse are the secrets and lies told to those who loved us because their effects are still in the present.

Now everyone will know Darby for what she is – a used sex-object. She'd allowed herself to be pawed and screwed by her father, and watched men jerk off in front of her. It wasn't the fact that it happened; it was who would let that happen to themselves? Certainly not a sixteen-year-old. What was I going to say when I got back to school?

On the last day of group, I leave with tears in my eyes because I know that some of the girls are not going to make it; they are likely to kill themselves. I was not 100% sure about myself either. The urge to leave still visited, especially at night.

Mom is coming tomorrow.

47

Mom

I wasn't sure if she needed time, or they thought I needed time. I wanted to see her but I didn't know what I was supposed to say. All I could think of, was that I couldn't bear Mom having to look into the face of a liar. Cathy told me not to worry, that moms are so glad you're still alive and it would be a while before we got to the why's and why-nots. I'd figure out what to say when I saw her.

I walk down with Annabella, to meet her. I shift my notebook left to right. I remember my list is on the back pages. We walk up to a window. A woman stands on the other side. Annabella's hand grasps me just above my elbow.

Mom wears a winter coat. Her left arm lies across her stomach and her right hand supports her chin. She rubs her face, turns and walks in a circle around the room. She looks through the window, but doesn't acknowledge me. I look quizzically at Annabella.

"She can't see you – it's a mirror."

I step forward. Annabella's hand leaves my arm. My mother looks right at me. She's no longer the tall, head-up woman I knew. She is well dressed and neat, but there's a sag. Three lines crease her forehead. Her lips are moving, like she is reciting a prayer. My mom, the woman that's been mistaken for my older sister, has turned into an old woman. I imagine Dad yelling at her, saying this was all her fault, and if she'd just minded her own fucking business the family would still be together. I think about telling Annabella that I can't see her now. That I want to go back to my room. In the next second, I know Mom is probably wishing the same.

"Are you ready, Darby? Your mom looks like she's anxious to see you."

"I'm ready." I reach for the knob, turn and push. Mom's eyes meet mine as she walks over to me and wraps me in her arms. I squeeze her as tight as I dare. My head fills with a scent. My mother.

"It's so great to see you!" she says into my hair. "I promised myself I wouldn't cry because I've done enough over the last days, and we can't talk if we're going to sit here and cry. The nurses tell me you're receiving some help, so am I, and things seem to be progressing. Darby, I'm so sorry."

"I know, Mom. Me too."

We sit on a couch. She holds my hand and starts with things she rehearsed. Dad is gone and they are getting a divorce. I decide not to ask where he went. She and Davey are at Aunt Mary's for the day, because the movers are at the house getting Dad's stuff. They'd be back home tomorrow. Mrs. Campbell, Aunt Mary, and Sally are coming over tomorrow to clean up after the movers. I can come home any time after that, whenever I am ready. There are going to be legal proceedings in the future. Davey is seeing a psychologist to help him cope with it all. "He told me to tell you he misses you. School called and they are going to work something out, whenever you are ready."

Then, I tell her what I had rehearsed. That I am sorry, and that I have no words to explain why I lied for so long. I tell her I'm relieved the lies are over. I say I am happy she came to see me, and I'm glad that she still wants me to come home. With that, her lips quiver. Her eyes fill with tears and overflow. She wraps me in a hug and keeps repeating, "Darby, I love you, I love you...."

"It's OK Mom, don't cry. I'm not going to leave." She sniffles and wipes away her tears. I sit back and show her my notebook.

"I've been keeping a notebook in group and with the psychologist. They said it might be beneficial for both of us if I shared some of the stuff." I flip the book open. I promise myself to read in a strong voice. I open to the sticky note, tilt the book so Mom can also see. Deep breath.

48

Listing Forward

I start reading.

"Graduate from high school." I look up and say, "Maybe finish this school year from home? We could look into that.

"Move back upstairs, if no one minds, at least for a while.

"Record myself playing my sax at the Buckleys.

"Tell Sara I'm sorry for the lies. She's not to blame for any of this and she needs to hear that from me.

"Take Driver ED. I have been driving for four years now, no tickets yet." I smile.

"Look into some postsecondary music programs.

"Start guitar lessons with Mom. It can't be that hard; you only need three chords.

"Teach Davey to play guitar, if he wants to learn.

"Go fishing with Mom.

"Never see or speak to *him* again. *That* might be hard.

"Take swimming lessons. I might be a lifeguard. That would be a good summer job.

"Keep seeing my psychologist.

"One day at a time."

Afterword

I wrote this novel over a period of ten years. Numerous people helped me, especially in the early days, in the creation of Darby. It all started with me writing with my Grade Nine students—they were my first editors.

It is the amateur editors' and readers' feedback that first-time authors get their inspiration from, and that moves you forward. There are a few who inspired me.

Special thanks to:

Lori Farren, Julia Mawer, Shane Buchanan, Bertis Sutton, and John Hanson.

My partner, Denise Connors, who worked through hours of drafts and edits, and who provided encouragement.

Saint John Voices for giving me a chance to read aloud.

The Write Cup Bookstore Café and Write Saint John writing group.

On the professional side:

The Writers' Federation of New Brunswick for validating the story through their writing contest.

Lee Thompson for the editing and for moving the story to submission level.

Galleon Press for taking the chance on a first-time author writing the 'Forbidden Story'.

Thomas

Thomas Chamberlain is a retired teacher. His career spanned 33 years. He taught elementary school in Plaster Rock and high school in Quispamsis, New Brunswick. His final three years prior to retirement were spent teaching Inuit children in a small community on the shores of Hudson's Bay. Throughout Thomas' career, he had a reputation for innovation and creativity in teaching.

Thomas enjoys the outdoors, and all the Maritimes has to offer. He has published articles on hunting and fishing in New Brunswick, and on training hunting dogs. Thomas co-created the World Pond Hockey Championships in Plaster Rock, New Brunswick.

Happenstance is his first novel. It was awarded 2nd place in the 2024 Writers' Federation of NB Writing Competition, in the David Adams Richards category for unpublished fiction.

He currently lives in the Kennebecasis Valley with his partner Denise and their Labrador Retriever, Islay.

www.thomas-chamberlain.com